AQUARIAN

JAN COFFEY

ISBN: 978-1479104574

AQUARIAN

Copyright © 2012 by Nikoo & James McGoldrick

All rights reserved. Except for use in any review or face-to-face educational use, the reproduction or utilization of this work in whole or in part in any form by any electronic, mechanical or other means, now known or hereafter invented, including xerography, photocopying and recording, or in any information storage or retrieval system, is forbidden without the written permission of the publisher:

M M Books
PO Box 665
Watertown, CT 06795

This is a work of fiction. Names, characters, places and incidents are either the product of the author's imagination or are used fictitiously, and any resemblance to actual persons, living or dead, business establishments, events or locales is entirely coincidental.

Printed in the United States of America
First US Edition 2012

Visit us on the Web:

www.JanCoffey.com

Art work: Kimberly Killion, Hot Damn Designs

There is...mystery about this sea, whose gently awful stirrings seem to speak of some hidden soul beneath.

—Herman Melville

CHAPTER 1

No cell phone service. No cable TV. No mall. No bars. No party scene. No Internet. No Facebook. No traffic to throw yourself in front of.

"What," Killian muttered, "am I getting myself into?"

Looking around in every direction from the small motor launch, she could see nothing. Darkness covered the Atlantic like the wing of some enormous black bird. No moon, no stars, no welcoming ray from any lighthouse or passing ship. Only an occasional lightning flash lit the invisible horizon before being instantly snuffed out.

The damp wind was cold. Killian pulled her Green Mountain Academy sweatshirt more tightly around her. She'd graduated only two weeks ago, but it felt like forever. She stared up at the silent old man at the wheel of the boat. In the darkness he was little more than a hunched silhouette, a pipe clenched in his teeth.

"How long before we reach Cuttylea Island?" she called out to him.

Thomas Eliot turned and looked back at her. Killian couldn't see his eyes, but saw his hand dip into his jacket pocket. He stuffed something into the pipe. With practiced skill he produced a lighter from somewhere. He lit the pipe again, revealing the deep lines of his weathered face.

"How long?" he replied finally. The end of the pipe glowed as he puffed. The smell of the tobacco whipped by her, mingling with the briny scent of the sea and fish and old bait. "An hour. Tops."

Everything that Killian feared was conspiring against her tonight. Night. Water. The distant lightning threatening ominously. She stared into the darkness to where ocean and sky ground together, producing those muffled flashes of light. The storm was approaching. She hated electrical storms at any time.

The thought of being caught in one—out on the open sea in this ancient floating coffin—held *no* appeal for her.

She shivered. What disturbed her most were the memories that went along with the storms. So many nights she'd spent at her mother's hospital bedside, looking out the sixth-floor window at Boston's city lights. Lightning had illuminated the skyline the night Killian had been told nothing more could be done for Ama's cancer. Rain from a thunderstorm had been pelting the windows when she'd died a week later.

That was four years ago. She couldn't change the past. What she had to think about was now. This summer. Come fall, she had no boarding school in Vermont to go back to. There was no college waiting for her, either. She hadn't applied to any.

Restless, Killian looked back at the wake left by the boat's engine.

A real ferry traveled between Hyannis and Cuttylea Island twice a week. The website said the crossing took three hours, one way. Killian hadn't been able to get to Cape Cod for the trip out to the island on either of those days. So here she was, plowing through the increasingly heavy seas of the dark Atlantic. On a boat no bigger than a pickup truck.

She heard the rumble of thunder over the steady roar of the boat's engines. Killian shivered again. She slid her butt along the wooden bench, moving closer to cockpit of the boat. Stretching up, she glanced ahead. The single headlight on the bow barely illuminated anything in their path. The dim light rising and dropping as the boat pitched forward into the growing swells did nothing to quell the uneasiness in her stomach.

"Do you think the storm will catch us before we reach the island?"

Thomas cocked his head and relit the pipe. Killian already knew there was no point in repeating the question. The old man wasn't much of a talker. Half of the questions Killian asked had gone unanswered.

Lightning suddenly lit the choppy, rolling sea. Almost immediately, thunder exploded around them like a sledge hammer on an empty drum. The boat vibrated from the concussion. Killian dove inside the backpack between her feet, frantically dragging out her iPod and earpieces. Plugging herself in, she was stunned when no sound came out. The screen was lit, but no music. She turned the device off and on and watched as the screen came back to life. Still nothing. Killian tore the earpieces away and stuffed everything back in her bag.

She was shivering uncontrollably now. Here it was, the first week in June, but she was freezing. Reaching back into the bag, she pulled out a windbreaker. It belonged to her father. She'd snatched it at the last minute on her way out of the house.

Some of the literature she'd printed out about Cuttylea Island came out with the jacket, flying free in the sharp wind. Dropping the garment, she grabbed for the loose pages. They were gone, sweeping over the stern and fluttering like falling snow into the dark sea. Killian stared after them. Picking up the windbreaker, she yanked it over her head. She could smell her father in it. She welcomed the added warmth.

Killian had still been at school a month ago when the invitation came. It was from her mother's great aunt, Hannah Winthrop. The note had asked her to come and spend the summer working on Cuttylea. At the time, Killian equated the offer with death by boredom. Three weeks later, reality reared its ugly head. She graduated and had to move back home.

Killian knew she wouldn't fit into her father's picture-perfect New England family. The new wife, the two-point-two kids, the dog, and the white picket fence. It was the family Rick had all too quickly constructed after her mother died. The picture didn't include her. From her first week in Middlebury, she'd felt like a weed in the suburban flower patch.

So Hannah's offer had begun to sound very attractive.

The rising and plunging of the boat was getting to Killian. At the top of each wave, her stomach lifted and hung in mid-air as the bow dipped and then dropped with a bang onto the next wave. Killian panicked. She hadn't told Thomas that she didn't know how to swim. She looked around. Not a lifejacket in sight.

Suddenly, the boat rocked as the driver cut the speed.

"What's wrong?"

Without a word, the old man swung the wheel and gunned the engine. The boat carved a sharp arc, forcing Killian to grip the side to keep from sliding off the bench.

As they came around, Thomas was peering just ahead and then over the side. Killian turned in her seat, looking down into the water.

Then he cut the engines and the boat stopped.

Her great aunt trusted this man. She'd sent him to Hyannis to get her. Or at least this was what Thomas had told Killian on the dock. Her mind now started questioning even that. She peered over the side, following his gaze.

Suddenly, a hand shot up from the dark waters. Before she could move, it was gripping the edge. Their fingers touched.

Killian gasped aloud and sprang backward. But there was nowhere to go. She tripped over her pack, landing hard against the bench running along the other side.

Her heart raced. The hand had been warm. Dead bodies don't reach up out of the water.

The boat rocked sharply. When she straightened and turned around, Killian was astounded to see a young man, a head taller than Thomas, standing in the boat. Her legs gave up and she sank down onto the bench. The old man had draped a blanket over the swimmer's shoulders.

His eyes were fixed on her. Killian felt her face flush hot under his steady gaze. Then the newcomer ducked down into the cabin space in the bow.

Thomas moved back behind the wheel and revved up the engines. The boat leapt forward, cutting through the waves.

"Who...who is that?"

"That's Perth," Thomas said over his shoulder. He pulled the pipe from between his teeth and banged out the contents on the side of the boat. "He's training to swim the channel."

"In this weath—?"

The old man cranked the wheel, turning the boat at full speed. Killian clutched the bench to keep from sliding into the sea.

For the first time, she noticed that it had begun to rain.

CHAPTER 2

Swimming the channel.

Names jumped at her. Cross Rip Channel. Muskeget Channel. Great Rip Channel. Killian couldn't remember which of them went with what island off Cape Cod, but she recalled reading about inter-island swim competitions.

What kind of idiot would be out swimming in a storm like this?

A handsome one, that's for sure.

She peered toward the door of the cabin where Perth had disappeared. She'd taken her suitcase down there earlier. The space hadn't been tall enough for her to stand in. Crammed with boat gear and fishing stuff, it smelled dank and fishy. She couldn't wait to come back into the open air.

Killian saw him emerge. As he came through the doorway, their gazes locked for a brief moment, and she felt a sudden jolt. Instinct told her to back away. Handsome or not, there was an intense, almost predatory look in the way he was sizing her up.

The blanket was gone. Perth was wearing a plain dark teeshirt that was too small for him. An old pair of shorts. She wondered if the clothes belonged to Thomas. His feet were bare. Standing next to the old man, Perth seemed unaffected by the rain and the cold bite of the wind.

Thomas leaned toward him and whispered. "She's the one."

Killian was surprised at the words.

Perth made no reply. He moved easily on the bouncing boat and sat down on the bench across from her. Suddenly, Killian felt crowded. His long legs stretched out, filling the space. She had nowhere to look but into his face, half-hidden in the darkness. What she could see were chiseled features, a straight nose, a strong chin. She couldn't guess his age. His hair was dark and on the long side. The wind was whipping it about his face. Her gaze moved downward. The shirt was stretched across the muscles of a broad chest. He made Michael Phelps look scrawny.

The boat hit the sea with an extra hard slap. Killian's forgotten backpack bounced down the deck. She grabbed for it. Perth put out a foot to stop the slide. She accidentally touched his leg before getting hold of the bag.

Strong and muscular legs, amazing chest, warm skin, a handsome face. He was all raw power. She felt flustered just noticing his body. She blamed it on spending the last four years at an all-girl boarding school. Killian yanked the bag between her feet. She forced her gaze back to his face without pausing anywhere along the way.

He was still staring.

"Hi, I'm Killian," she shouted. "I can't believe you were swimming in this."

Before she could finish, a clap of thunder exploded practically in her head, causing her to jump. The boat's pitch and roll were becoming more severe. She looked over her shoulder as a branching bolt of lightning streaked down, burying its tips in the sea not far away. Another thunderous blast immediately followed the light show. The storm was almost on top of them.

Killian felt insignificant as nature slapped the boat every which way. She had no control over what was going to happen to them.

"I don't know how to swim," she called out over the noise of the storm.

Perth gave no sign that he'd heard her, but Thomas turned and motioned to Killian. "Life vests are in the storage space under your seat."

She scrambled to her feet, trying to keep her balance. She opened the compartment and offered the first vest to Thomas. He never turned, but waved a dismissive hand, letting her know he didn't need one.

The boat suddenly became airborne for a couple of seconds. It smashed down on the water with enough force to throw Killian across the narrow deck. She landed against Perth. Strong hands grabbed her by the waist and helped her to right herself. She held out the life vest to him. He tossed it back into the bin.

"Okay, drown. Both of you," she said. Moving unsteadily, she hauled the life vest out again. In a moment, she was pulling the straps tight.

Two shirts, a heavy sweatshirt, windbreaker, the life vest. Killian felt as big as a Goodyear blimp. But it didn't matter.

They were going to die. The waves around them loomed high over the boat. She struggled to close the storage bin. Perth reached around her leg and closed it. She sat down, her hands searching for something to hold on to. Seawater broke over the side and smacked Killian across the back, drenching her and sending her sliding down the bench and onto the deck.

There was no point in trying to get back to her seat. The boat was hitting one wave after another, and they were airborne between the collisions. She huddled in the corner against the fishing gear.

The next dive through the air was hell. Killian felt her stomach lurch. She grabbed a bait bucket. The smell of dead fish finished the job. Her stomach emptied.

But that was only the beginning. The world as she knew it was coming to an end. She couldn't stop heaving. Sharp cramps, nausea, the helplessness of being thrown around the deck actually made drowning sound like a death she could live with.

The storm was getting stronger, the sea rougher, her stomach more determined to punish her. She couldn't stop shivering. Each time the boat rose and landed, she struggled to stay put. Killian wrapped her arms around the foul bait bucket, dreading the next wave.

A large hand took hold of her wrist. Strong fingers slipped beneath the cuff of the windbreaker and sweatshirt, touching her skin. Shock, pleasure, comfort, an assortment of sensations rushed through her, all having to do with the realization that she wasn't alone. Someone was taking care of her. Perth had slid down the bench and was leaning over.

"Feel free to throw me overboard."

Her weak attempt at humor didn't register with him. His fingers remained locked around her wrist. He didn't pull her up onto the bench. He didn't say anything to calm her nerves. But there was something about the touch. A feeling of warmth from his fingers slowly seeped into her. Her stomach's violent protests eased. Thoughts of impending death disappeared. Even her fear lessened. She let go of the bucket.

Killian struggled to come up with a rational explanation.

"Pressure points?" she managed to ask. "I've read about that for motion sickness."

Killian pushed herself away from the bucket and fishing gear. She leaned back against the bench Perth was sitting on. The storm wasn't letting up. She peered at the waves and the lightning. She was no longer afraid.

"Hypnotism, maybe," she muttered. "Better than Dramamine. You could make a lot of money bottling this stuff."

The howl of the wind was her answer.

She chuckled absently, amused by her own talkativeness. She looked at her wrist, caught in his grip. His skin was darker than hers. She studied the line of his knuckles. She felt the pressure of his thumb. He seemed to control her pulse, the very beating of her heart.

Killian rested her shoulder against his knee. She suddenly felt tired, drowsy. Nothing bothered her. She had no fears. She leaned her head against his leg and closed her eyes.

Killian was swimming, so she knew it must be a dream. She was miles offshore. She wasn't afraid. Stroke after stroke, she pulled herself smoothly, powerfully through the sea. The water was warm, caressing her body. She could hear music. Strange music. She felt free. She was in search of something. Someone.

"Perth." Killian opened her eyes, uncertain if she called his name aloud or in her sleep. The sky was dark. It was raining. But the waters were calm. She looked across the way and saw lights from the shore. They were in a harbor.

The edge of the bench was digging into her back. She was soaked to the bone. She stretched and weakly hauled herself onto the bench. Thomas was steering the boat toward a dock near a cluster of small houses. Looking back, she saw flashes of lightning beyond a line of rocks that formed a breakwater.

"Cuttylea Island," Thomas said aloud. "We're home."

Killian peered past him into the darkness of the cabin. No one was there.

Perth was gone.

CHAPTER 3

"And where have you been all my life?" Hannah Winthrop put her cup of tea down next to the sink. She took Killian into her arms. "It's not right for someone as young as you to have gone through so much."

Killian ignored the lump in her chest. She wasn't going to revisit the past again. Not tonight. She was just thankful for being here now.

Hannah was standing beside an old green golf cart at the dock when Thomas tied his boat up. She showed more enthusiasm at seeing her than any of Killian's other relatives—including her father or his parents—ever showed.

From what Killian could tell, the island boasted only two paved roads. One ran along the edge of the harbor and the other ran uphill from the dock. Almost at the top, the road split into several branches. One was a dirt lane leading to the wood-shingled cottage where Hannah lived. The island had no streetlights. No cars that she could see. No one was out walking when they tied up at the dock.

Once in the house, Hannah ordered Killian to take a hot shower and change. And by the time she stood at the top of the stairs, pulling her wet hair back in a ponytail, the smell that greeted Killian made her think she might actually eat something.

A cup of clam chowder, homemade oatmeal cookies, and hot chocolate convinced her. Sitting together at the kitchen table, Hannah went on about how happy she was to have Killian here and how this reminded her of the summers that Ama had spent on the island as a teenager.

"Thank you for making me feel so welcome, Aunt Hannah," Killian said now, pulling out of the embrace.

"Don't start with any *Aunt* Hannah. I'm just Hannah."

Killian smiled. As she dried the dishes, she listened to the rain and the howling wind battering against the walls. The storm had finally reached the island. She was glad to be inside, safe and warm.

"My mother always talked about the summers she spent here."

"Yes. Yes, those were special days," Hannah said. She took the clean dishes from Killian and stacked them on the shelf. "But you'll soon find out for yourself that coming here is like stepping back in time. Not much has changed since the last time Ama was here."

And the same could be said of Hannah. She had seen many pictures of the old woman with teenaged Ama. Gray hair. Wrinkled, sun-kissed skin. She'd looked so full of life in the photos. She looked the same way now.

"Why was it that my mother never brought me here?"

Hannah always sent birthday and Christmas cards and homemade presents. But Killian only met Hannah twice before. Both instances were crystal clear in her mind. The first time was when her mother was hospitalized for a week after an early cancer treatment in Boston. The second time was at her funeral three years later.

Hannah shook her head sadly. "She went where your father wanted to go, lived where he chose, vacationed where he decided. Life on the island can be a jolt for workaholics. I don't think Rick could have lasted a day just doing nothing here."

That was still true. He had his new wife, his new children, his dog, but he didn't spend enough time with them. Killian still remembered that in four years of boarding school, he'd not once shown up for a Parent's Weekend.

Killian looked around the cozy kitchen. Everything had its place. Glass front cupboards with plates and bowls and glasses. Mugs dangling from hooks. On a shelf, a creamer and sugar set decorated with the hand-painted figure of a little mermaid. An old fashioned clock on the wall.

One large room and one small one that opened off the kitchen made up the entire downstairs. The front door of the house was clearly never used, and was blocked by furniture in the living room. Beneath the kitchen, a small cellar had shelves filled with bottles of jam and pickles. Upstairs, two bedrooms were separated by a bathroom with a claw-footed tub.

"I can't wait for you to show me around the island," Killian said happily.

"Tomorrow morning, we'll do just that. Now wait...are you one of those young people whose morning is really the middle of the afternoon?"

"I can sleep in with the best of them," she said honestly. "But not when I'm at school, working, or having a life. I can get up anytime you start your day."

Hannah chuckled. "I'm not that cruel, honey. How about if we aim at midday sometime, or whenever you roll out of bed? I talked to Elena at the inn. She doesn't expect you to start at the job until the day after tomorrow."

Killian saw this as her cue to ask about Perth. Thomas had said nothing more on the boat after she'd found the swimmer missing, and it had felt awkward asking Hannah about it earlier. She leaned against the fridge.

"On the boat ride over..." Killian stopped, hearing footsteps outside. Someone was at the kitchen door.

"You were saying?" Hannah encouraged.

There was a knock.

"This must be Perth. I asked him this morning to stop by tonight. That boy never passes up an invitation for my cookies."

Panic, embarrassment, the sudden flip in her stomach were totally confusing. Killian had been ready to ask about him a moment before. But now, as her great aunt reached for the door, she had to fight the urge to run upstairs and hide.

Killian glanced down at her clothes. She was dressed in a sweatshirt and sweatpants. Pink ones from a breast cancer rally, at that. Her black hair was tied up in a ponytail. No make up. And when she'd checked in the mirror upstairs, her normally pale skin still had a greenish tinge from the boat ride over. There were dark circles under her eyes. In the best of circumstances, she was far from being a beauty. She was definitely making no fashion statement tonight.

The kitchen door swung open. He stepped in, bringing with him the smell of night and the storm.

Killian wedged herself against the side of the fridge. Perth leaned down and pecked Hannah on the cheek.

"Smells great in here."

He had a deep voice, too. Killian realized she shouldn't have expected anything less. He was a perfect specimen. He was wearing different shorts and a clean tee-shirt, but still had bare feet. His back was to her and she admired his broad shoulders and height. The rain had speckled his shirt, but he didn't seem to notice.

"Hannah, do you mind if I get my plate of cookies to go? Walt needs me tonight."

"Of course you can, hon. But not before I introduce you to my grandniece." Hannah stepped past him, and his attention swung around to Killian.

Butterflies dancing in the stomach. Heartbeat racing. Going soft in the knees. Her skin burning. And she had an almost overwhelming desire to run away.

His gaze met hers with the same intensity that she felt on the boat. It was the look of the wolf silently sizing up its next meal.

She forgot how to speak.

"Killian Ama Fitch," Hannah said cheerfully, obviously unaware of the tension in the kitchen. "She'll be staying with me for the summer and working at the inn, doing whatever Elena wants her to do."

"We met on Thomas's boat," Perth said in a low voice. "She doesn't have her sea legs. She also doesn't know how to swim."

He made it sound like not liking water was a cardinal sin, Killian thought.

"Well, that's something that you can help her out with." Hannah turned to Killian. "Perth swims competitively and gives classes to some of the summer folks who vacation on the island."

"We'll see," he said, turning abruptly to the older woman. "I have to go."

"I know. I know. Here's your plate of cookies. You tell Walt that I'll stop by and check on him tomorrow."

Killian, rooted in the same spot, watched the two chat and move toward the door. She couldn't understand the reason for his obvious coolness. He could have at least tried to be civil.

Hannah closed the door behind him and turned to Killian. "Perth and his father live next door. Walt is a paraplegic and a widower. He brought the boy to the island after his wife died in the same accident that put him in the wheelchair. They both can be gruff and bossy at times. But they're good people."

Killian had no doubt the last couple of sentences were for her benefit. She'd met and dealt with plenty of brusque people in her life. The real problem was that she'd never before been so tongue-tied and wobbly at the sight of any boy.

Hannah patted her on the arm. "He's slow to warm up to new faces. Perth's a little older, but you two are close enough in age that I'm betting you'll find a few things you have in common. You're going to get along just fine. You'll see."

Killian already knew what she would have to do for them to 'get along just fine.' She would avoid him and spare herself any further embarrassment.

CHAPTER 4

Killian lifted herself on one elbow and looked out the window next to the bed. With the sun just above the distant horizon, the sight was breathtaking.

Undulating hills of green grass sloped down to a horseshoe shaped harbor. A half dozen cottages were visible from her vantage point, as well as a few more houses crowded around the town dock. A small lighthouse sat on a stone breakwater by the entrance of the harbor.

Because of Hannah's welcome, Killian had a different view of what her summer here would be like. She already decided that she'd work hard and make some money. She might even indulge in her one hobby, painting. She'd always been a loner. Now that she was here, she realized this place would fit her personality like a glove.

She looked over at the bedside clock. It was only 5:45. She couldn't remember ever waking up this early without an alarm. But sleeping last night had been a challenge. She'd drifted in and out of strange dreams. There were noises all around her. The thunder rolling away into the distance, the slap of the water breaking over sand and rocks, music, the urgent whispers of people. Footsteps. Lots of footsteps. She couldn't hush the sounds in her head.

Killian stretched and tried to open the bedside window, but she couldn't get it done lying down. Climbing out of bed, she pulled it open. The window slid up easily.

No screen. The clean sea air washed over her.

Killian leaned out and filled her lungs. From this view she saw four other cottages lined the narrow dirt lane that Hannah's house sat on. Of different sizes and shapes, they all sported the same gray, weather-beaten shingles. Spaced far enough apart to offer privacy, not one cottage obstructed the ocean view of any other.

She looked off the other way. Only one house was visible before the lane disappeared into the woods. The handicap ramp leading to the door at the side of the house told her the cottage must belong to Perth and his father.

Perth. She pulled her head back in. She didn't want to start thinking about him this early in the morning.

The bedroom was small and the angles of the roof cut into her headroom. A bed, a dresser, a small table next to the bed, and an old rocking chair were the only furnishings. An antique patchwork quilt was hanging on the wall next to the bed. An oval braided rug covered most of the wide planks of wood flooring. A wooden chest containing extra blankets sat at the foot of her bed. Killian guessed that little if anything had changed from the days when her mother summered here.

Killian's open suitcase sat on the floor, taking up most of the space on the rug. She'd put a few of her clothes in the dresser last night.

She opened the narrow closet door now and looked inside. Beyond the short bar for hanging clothes, the storage space went far back under the eaves. Killian peered at the neatly stacked boxes deep in the gloom. She wondered if Hannah had anything of her mother's.

These days, Killian was desperate to find things belonging to Ama. At her father's house she'd been told bluntly not to ask questions or even bring her name up. It might upset Susan, the new wife. No pictures of Ama or anything of hers remained in that house. Killian's father acted as if no other woman had ever existed in his life before Susan.

Killian hated that. Her mother's memory had been pushed like a worn shirt to the back of a drawer.

She still kept one photo album. She cherished it, along with the handful of pictures that she'd taken to boarding school with her. All that was left of Ama seemed to exist in those photos.

The morning air blowing in was cool on her skin. Pulling on a sweatshirt, she took her clothes out of the suitcase and laid them on the bed. She knelt down again. A towel protected the treasures beneath. She took out the frames one by one and started arranging them on the dresser and the small bedside table.

The distant murmur of voices coming from outside drew Killian to the window. She looked out. There was no one in sight.

Time...

Alone...

Killian...

This wasn't her imagination. She was hearing voices. She stared at the empty lane and the grass glistening with last night's rain.

And then she saw the first people coming along the lane from the line of the trees. Others followed, emerging from the shadows of the woods into the early morning light.

Considering the early hour, she was surprised by the numbers. Forty? Fifty? As far as she could tell, this could have been almost everyone on the island. Their ages seemed to range in from middle-aged to ancient. She recognized Thomas, the man who'd ferried her out. Then she spotted Hannah pushing a man in a wheelchair. The two of them turned in at the ramp next door. Perth's father, Walt.

Even from her place at the window, Killian sensed that the mood of the approaching group was quite somber. There was no sign of Perth. She watched as her great aunt stood for a few moments, talking to Walt.

She backed away from the window, watching the group pass by.

A sunrise service? A group meditation? Some Tai Chi session? Maybe this was what people did early in the morning on an island where the sidewalks were rolled up at sunset. That is, if they had sidewalks.

Killian quickly put away the rest of her belongings. Now that she knew Hannah was up, she was eager to get a head start on the day. Picking up her iPod, she threw it into one of the drawers. She'd checked it again last night. Dead.

As she hung clothes in the closet, Killian thought how strange it was not to be checking email or Facebook. Not to be texting. That was all part of her everyday morning routine. Killian had already checked her phone. There was no cell service.

Operating at the other end of technological spectrum, Hannah didn't even have an old-fashioned landline phone. She told Killian last night the summer crowd had ways of getting service for their computers and cell phones, but she didn't understand any of it.

Back in Hyannis, Killian had called her father and told him she was at the Cape and taking a boat over. He'd asked her to call him in a week's time to report on how she was doing. This was the usual extent of their communication. Once a week reporting, no matter where she was or what she was doing. She hung up his windbreaker on a hook by the door where she could see it every day.

Killian was showered, dressed, and ready to face the day in less than an hour. The smell of fresh-brewed coffee and bacon drew her straight to the kitchen. She stood in the doorway, closed her eyes for a second, and inhaled deeply before letting out a satisfied sigh.

"Breakfast. My favorite meal of the day."

"Good," Hannah said, looking over her shoulder from the stove. "That makes two of you."

"Two?"

"Two. Have a seat, honey." She waved a spatula toward the table.

Killian fought the urge to step back.

Perth was standing by the table with forks and knives in his hands. He paused and glanced at her. The same aloof expression she'd seen last night. She tried to imagine him looking different than he did. Beady little pig eyes or a crooked, broken nose or a huge zit in the middle of his forehead. *Anything* to lessen the fact that he looked this good so early in the morning. Impossible. It didn't seem to matter. Perth was just plain hot, in a very discomforting kind of way.

Her gaze narrowed. He was also like the proverbial bad penny. He kept turning up. She walked past him to Hannah and kissed the old woman's cheek.

"Can I help you with breakfast?"

"You can start some toast," Hannah replied, motioning toward the counter.

Killian waited for Perth to finish taking plates out of the cabinet above the toaster. His broad shoulders filled the space in the kitchen. He even smelled good. She forced her attention back to Hannah. "So, did you have a nice walk this morning?"

"Walk?" She hesitated for only an instant. "Oh, I haven't been out today. Perth tells me it's a nice day."

Killian paused, surprised and unsure how to respond to the denial. She stared at Hannah's back. She couldn't imagine why the older woman would lie to her about something so unimportant.

"I…"

Killian stopped, feeling Perth's eyes on her.

"I must have been dreaming," she said, pushing past him to the toaster.

"You were pretty tired last night," her great aunt said brightly.

Killian put bread into the toaster and watched the wires grow red. She hadn't been dreaming. Old people *did* forget things. She remembered the last time she'd gone with her father to see her grandmother. She couldn't even remember Killian's name. As soon as the toast popped up, she put in two more slices of bread.

Minutes later, the three sat down at the table. Eggs, bacon, toast, coffee. Life was good, with the exception of the silent hulk sitting across from her. Killian tried not to look at him, tried not to touch his hand as they passed plates or when they both reached for the salt and pepper at the same time. She tried not to stare, even though his eyes were the most beautiful shade of green in the bright sunlight pouring into the kitchen. His overnight growth of beard made him look even more handsome.

Thankfully, Hannah talked enough for the three of them, keeping any awkward pauses to a minimum.

Halfway through breakfast, there was a knock. Hannah quickly rose to answer it herself.

"Good morning." The caller didn't come in, but Killian could hear the man's gravelly voice.

Hannah stepped out, partly closing the door behind her.

"We have to get started. Use me as an excuse, if you need to, but send them on their way."

"Wait. She's already…"

Hannah pulled the door closed.

Perth reached across the table for the bottle of jam. His fingers accidentally brushed against hers. Killian quickly placed her hand on her lap.

"Do you know who that is at the door?" she asked, trying to cover the awkwardness of the moment.

"Of course." He stretched his legs under the table until his bare toes touched hers.

She tucked her feet under the chair. "So, who is he?"

"You don't know him."

Killian watched him get up and pour himself more coffee. His bare arm brushed against her shoulder when he filled her cup. She shifted in the chair, feeling her cheeks catch fire. "I don't know *anyone* on the island."

There was a hint of amusement in the handsome face when he sat down again.

Killian added too much sugar to her coffee and made a production of stirring it. She had no clue if this gorgeous hunk was making moves on her or not. He was totally out of her league.

She looked up. He was studying her face.

"Why are you afraid of me?" he asked.

"Afraid? That's ridiculous. I'm not afraid of you."

He leaned across the table; she sat back involuntarily.

"I mean it. What are you afraid of?"

"I am *not* afraid." Killian couldn't tell the truth. She wouldn't admit that she'd finished high school without ever having a real boyfriend. She wouldn't confess that she was more accustomed to being invisible to specimens like him. "But seriously. I haven't been here for a day, and I've seen you more than I've seen Hannah."

Killian's face felt like it was about to burst into flames. The tips of her ears were burning. This 'fight or flight' reflex was totally new. Usually, it was just flight. She forced herself to get it together.

"Really," she said, trying to lighten her tone. "Don't you have a home of your own? Can't you make your own breakfast? You were here last night. What are you doing here this morning?"

"Hannah asked me to come here last night *and* this morning." His gaze never wavered from her face. A touch of amusement crept into his expression. "I figured you must be a handful. Just trying to help her out."

This was pathetic. It was like her friends trying to get her a date for the Formal last year. It was embarrassing to think her aunt worried about her.

"Look, you don't have to bother," Killian said. "I'll talk to her. I don't need anyone to look after me or keep me company. I'm fine on my own."

The older woman came back into the kitchen.

"Daniel needs me to work at the Town Hall this morning," she said, turning to Killian. "Daniel Sawyer is our police officer, fire chief, mayor, and postmaster. We wear a lot of hats here on the island. So today I'm helping him get the tax bills ready for the summer people."

"I can help," Killian offered.

"No need, honey." Hannah rested a hand on Perth's shoulder. "Would you be an angel and take our girl around town this morning and introduce her to folks? I promised last night I'd do that myself, but my morning has just filled up."

He paused before answering and stared across the table. Killian spoke up quickly.

"Actually, I was thinking I'd just take the morning and explore the island on my own."

"But—" Hannah started to protest.

"Two miles long, a mile across. Right?" Killian said cheerfully. "There's no way I can get lost. I'll be back by midafternoon, and if you're done with the tax bills, you can take me around yourself. How's that sound?"

Getting up from the table, she started clearing the plates before her aunt could try to talk her out of it. It was all settled.

CHAPTER 5

Killian was lost.
Everything looked the same. The trees. The rolling hills of grass. The white and yellow and purple wildflowers. The absence of any other human being since she'd left the house more than two hours ago.

The dirt lane she'd taken from Hannah's house into the woods almost immediately divided into a number of paths. She chose the middle one. Not long after, the path she was on reached another fork. She went left. And there were more forks. Pretty soon, Killian had no clue if she was crossing the island or circling around in the center of it. She'd seen no sign of the ocean in over an hour, and the high trees and noon sun offered little help as far as direction. Despite going to school in the mountainous wilds of Vermont, she was not too good at orienteering.

"Okay, I'm on an island. So where is the water?" she said out loud.

A grazing doe lifted her head some ten yards away and looked at her curiously. A rabbit trotted across the path. Killian was sure he had a smirk on his face.

"This is ridiculous," she muttered. "If I walk in one direction, I *have* to hit water sometime."

Killian looked around her as she took the last sip from her water bottle. No direction looked more promising than any other. Still, she was glad she'd come alone. This was an adventure, and she wasn't particularly worried. Not yet, anyway. And she definitely wasn't sorry about deciding not to tag along after Perth. She wasn't a charity case.

"I am *not* sorry," Killian yelled.

She looked around her at the trees. She needed to climb one. Dropping her backpack on the grass, she stripped off her sweatshirt and stuffed it in the bag.

"Two miles across, one mile wide," she repeated the words aloud, taking comfort in her own voice.

Killian spotted a tree that looked manageable to climb.

"Okay. A child could do this."

Stretching up, reaching, sliding down, banging her elbow, getting her hair tangled in a branch. Eventually, she succeeded in getting both feet off the ground and climbed upward. Ten feet up and exhausted, Killian admitted that a child would have done better. But she wasn't helpless, either. She'd done four years of sports in high school. She was no varsity athlete, to be sure, but she wasn't a total geek.

By the time Killian climbed high enough that she could see over the immediate tree tops, she was sweating and had a couple of nasty scratches. Standing on a branch, she peeled off her tee-shirt and threw it down.

Rolling up the bottom of her tank top, she leaned back against the tree trunk and took a breather, enjoying the touch of the breeze on her skin.

Even this high up, there was still no sign of the water. Through the leaves and not too far off to her right, Killian spotted the notched stone parapet of what looked to be the tower of an old castle. Jogging her memory, she recalled the building being on the opposite end of the island from the village. The online brochure imaginatively referred to it as 'The Tower.' No one seemed to know when it was built or by whom, but the old stone structure—which happened to be on the highest point on the island, had been last used by the Navy during WWII to watch for German U-boats.

Climbing down the tree was almost as physically demanding as going up. By the time both feet hit the ground, she had a new cut on her chin.

Killian found her shirt and shoved it into her backpack. Keeping the direction of the Tower in mind, she set off again.

The ground rose steadily. After ten minutes of working her way through the thinning brush, Killian spotted the stone structure through the trees.

"Thank God," she said, letting out a sigh of relief.

A moment later, she was out of the woods and climbing a grassy hill dotted with clumps of purple-flowered thistles. Killian dropped her backpack when she reached the building.

The gray stone structure was perched at the very edge of a cliff overlooking the water. It was definitely old. The round tower was more than two stories high. At the top she could see the castle-like notches she'd spotted from the tree. Ivy covered a lot of it, framing the openings of several windows.

Tall grass grew out of cracks in the rock slabs of the walkway encircling the tower, and Killian started around. At the base of one side, she found an arched doorway. Someone had nailed it closed with old plywood, crisscrossed by battered boards.

Killian continued around to the ocean side of the tower. She went to the cliff edge and looked down.

A few boulders and bushes protruding from the face of the cliff were the only thing between her and a large cove below. Instinctively, she moved back from the edge. She was no good at guessing heights, but it had to be over a hundred feet to the water. It was definitely high enough that this was no spot for thrill seekers who liked to jump off cliffs.

Killian looked along the line of the shore. She could see no houses on this side of the island. A thin strip of rock and sand bordered the far side of the cove. The only sign of life was a single freighter far off on the horizon.

I told you to go away and not come back.

Killian spun on her heel. There was no one there. Only the ivy-covered tower. The one open window facing her was dark and empty.

You gave me your word.

"Who are you? Where are you?"

I warned you. And you promised me.

She was hearing things. Her heart pounded. Invisible fingers of fear slipped around her throat.

"What?" she managed to murmur.

The hoarse cry of a sea gull startled her. She turned her head to see the bird fifty yards along the cliff disappear below the edge. Hearing steps, she spun back toward the Tower.

Killian gasped.

An old man. He'd come out of the Tower, or maybe materialized out of thin air. Whichever it was, he was coming directly toward her.

Dressed in a ragged jacket and pants, he was filthy. Long, matted gray beard. Thin, greasy hair fell to his shoulders. He was holding a walking stick that he swept in front of him as he walked. The smell of unwashed clothes and smoke reached her. His eyes, encased in deep wrinkles, were glazed. He was blind.

"Stop right there."

"Why, Ama?" he asked in a voice rusty with lack of use.

Killian stared.

"Ama? I'm not Ama," she finally replied. "That was my mother."

He said nothing.

"I'm Killian," she continued hurriedly. "I'm related to Hannah Winthrop. I'm staying on the island for the summer."

The man took a step closer. He was terrifying.

"Who are you?" she asked.

The old eyes clearly saw nothing, but she could feel them probing her mind. He lifted his walking stick and struck the ground with the end. It sounded like a clap of thunder, and Killian glanced down at it in surprise.

"Leave. You must leave the island."

She looked up as he lifted the walking stick and pointed it at her chest.

"Go! Now!"

Killian took one step back and fell.

Her arms flailed helplessly. Landing shoulder first on a protruding ledge, she felt the breath knocked from her lungs. And she was again falling through space.

After what felt like an eternity, Killian hit the water like a stone.

CHAPTER 6

Stunned by the fall, Killian continued to sink.

Gazing upward toward the retreating light at the surface, she did not feel any panic. Far from it, the usual fear that controlled her when she was in the water was replaced by something else.

Peace. Calm.

Drifting downward with the sounds of the undersea world in her ears, Killian felt a tranquility that warmed her. Not far away, she saw the shadowy edge of the cove. Clusters of mussels clung to rock. Branches of sea kelp waved in the soft currents, caressing her skin as she passed. She looked back up at the receding light. It was becoming less distinct, less significant with each passing second. Her black hair, freed from the ponytail, floated around her face.

This felt like a dream. A total separation from what she'd known as reality. The thought came to her that perhaps she was dead. She raised her hand in front of her eyes. A cloud of red followed the movement of her fingers. She was bleeding. She must be alive, she decided.

Killian gently hit the soft sandy bottom of the cove.

And then he was there. Perth.

Killian saw him swimming toward her. She didn't think a more beautiful creature existed. He was wearing no shirt. His hair streamed back from his face. She saw the look of alarm in his eyes. She wanted to tell him everything was fine. She was no longer afraid.

Moving behind her, Perth slipped one arm across her chest, lifted her off the bottom of the cove, and pushed toward the surface.

Regret. She couldn't understand where that feeling came from or why, but that was clearly what washed through her as they neared the top.

The moment they broke the surface, Killian gasped for breath. Air. There was plenty of it, but she didn't know how to fill her lungs. Like a fish out of water, she twisted in his grasp, fighting Perth to let her go. His arm was a steel band around her, keeping her captive as he swam toward the shore.

"Breathe, Killian. Breathe."

In panic she fought him, thrashing her legs and trying to turn in his arms. He continued to speak to her in a soothing voice. Encouraging her to breathe.

Then, when he'd dragged her near enough to the shore that she could feel her feet touch the stony sand, Killian started coughing up salt water. He didn't let her go. Holding her up, he helped her onto a narrow beach a short distance from the base of the cliff.

When they stepped out, a bolt of clarity about what had just happened struck her. And with it came excruciating, stabbing pains through her back, her right shoulder and arm. She looked up at the Tower. The notched ramparts were just visible above the top edge of the cliff. Killian shuddered, realizing how far she'd fallen.

It was a miracle that she was alive.

The thin stretch of sandy beach was a stone's throw from where she'd fallen. Her knees gave out. She winced, realizing she couldn't move her right arm. Her shoulder and elbow were pointing forward at an odd angle.

"Lie down," he ordered, helping her stretch out.

Every inch of her body hurt. Killian continued to cough with each breath she took.

"Breathe." Perth flattened his palm on her stomach, just below her breasts. "Breathe, Killian."

Warmth began to spread through her chest, her lungs. The coughing spasms subsided. She succeeded in taking in a breath of air. In a moment her body stopped protesting. She felt cold when he took his hand away.

Perth leaned over her. His fingers moved with feathery softness over the skin of her face, her neck, shoulders, and arms. He was checking for injuries. Killian's stomach twisted deliciously, despite the pain. She was cold and warm. Terrified and tranquil. She studied the muscles of his naked chest and abs, his strong arms, his beautiful face. She knew her wet tank top was stretched like a second skin on her chest. She blushed, feeling naked. She was helpless.

Doctors. Hospital. She had to get Perth to take her for x-rays. Killian was certain she had broken bones. Perhaps she had internal bleeding or other complications. She lifted her head off the sand and tried to sit up. Pain shot through her back.

"Stay," he said, pressing a palm against her shoulder.

Rather than pain, warmth spread from the touch of his hand. Killian closed her eyes as he cupped her collarbone, pressing ever so gently. Her mind struggled to understand. She waited for the physical response to the abuse her body had gone through to kick her out of this serenity. But it didn't come.

"Reiki?" she asked.

"Just relax. Let me fix you."

Killian opened her eyes and looked into his face. "Fix me? You can fix me?"

"I can if you let me."

"This is creepy." She squinted up past his serious face at the Tower high above. "I just fell...how far is that? Two hundred, three hundred feet? A half mile?"

Perth's hand moved to her shoulder. He pressed on the joint, and she prepared herself to cry out in pain. But there was only numbness and that crazy sensation of heat. With one hand still on her shoulder, he took hold of her wrist and gently pulled it away from her body. She heard two popping sounds, and he placed her arm on the sand.

"Those sounds can't be good."

Killian didn't want to move.

"Don't you think I should be seeing a doctor?" she asked. "I hit half a dozen rocks on the way down."

Perth was all concentration. His strong, warm fingers slid along her arm and tingles moved deep into her belly. Excitement and fear about what he was doing to her were waging a full-fledged battle. She needed a barrier. Some façade of control.

"I must be bleeding to death, too. I cut my arm."

He didn't talk. She had to carry the conversation for both of them.

"Are you wondering why I jumped off that cliff?"

"You jumped?"

She'd broken his concentration. "No. Not really. It was an accident. But I got scared and took a step back. That's how I fell."

"Scared? I wasn't even up there!"

"A sense of humor. Funny."

He didn't smile, but the creases in the corners of his eyes revealed his amusement. Killian watched him bend and straighten her right arm. She was no longer surprised that there was no pain.

"How do you do this?" she asked.

"What scared you up there?"

"An old guy dressed in rags. He came out of nowhere. I think he was blind. He was carrying a walking stick, anyway. He called me by my mother's name. He was saying things that made no sense."

"That's Lynx," Perth said. "He lives out here."

"He lives in the Tower?"

"No, near it. He has a shack not too far away. By the town dump." He took her elbow. "Roll over. I want to check your back."

"You mean fix my back," Killian said, glad to comply. Words couldn't describe his touch. She rolled onto her stomach in the sand, and there was only the slightest twinge of pain along her spine.

"Am I dead?" she asked, meaning it.

"No, you're not dead."

"I should be."

"Sorry," he replied. "But you're not."

She knew she wasn't really dead. A dead person wouldn't be sighing with contentment as he made the pain go away. "Then tell me how you do this."

"Why did you come out to the Tower? How did you find it?" He was changing the topic.

"Actually, I was lost."

He didn't laugh at her. His fingers dug into her spine, and she stifled a moan of satisfaction at the sensation that spread through the joints. The pain was totally gone.

"Okay, now tell me."

"Tell you what?"

"How you're doing this?"

There was the touch again along her spine. The numbing warmth that soothed her body.

"I know I sound like a broken record. But I should be a goner. At least, broken up into a dozen pieces." Killian lifted her face off the sand. "What are you? Who are you?"

"You talk too much."

"Maybe. But you don't talk enough." She tried to look at him over her shoulder, but his hand was moving upward along her backbone.

He wrapped one hand around the back of her neck, and she felt something going on in her head. Her worries were gone. All the concerns nagging at her just seconds ago were now history. Her cheek rested on the sand again.

She dozed, but for how long she didn't know.

When she opened her eyes again, she simply accepted Perth's ability to fix her.

"I left my backpack at the Tower. Somehow I have to go back up there and get it."

"I'll go up with you."

"Is he—Lynx—is he crazy?"

"I don't think so. Everyone on the island says he's harmless." There was a pause as his fingers moved down her spine and touched the bare skin between her tank top and her shorts. Her skin sizzled. "I don't know him myself. Lynx doesn't talk."

Killian was going to say that the old man had talked to her. But there was something else happening to her. His fingers were circling a spot on her lower back. The sensation was overwhelming.

"How did you get this?"

His voice was thicker. Killian knew what he was asking about. The star-shaped mark near the base of her spine. A pentagram.

"It's not a tattoo," she explained. That's what most of her friends thought it was. "It's a birthmark. I've always had it."

Killian shivered as he caressed the spot.

Abruptly, he tapped her on the shoulder and stood up.

"I guess you'll live," he said brusquely. "Let's climb back up to the Tower and get your stuff."

CHAPTER 7

No broken bones, no bloody cuts, no tender-to-the-touch bruises. No pain at all from what she'd gone through. She was perfectly fine.

Killian followed Perth up the path. They climbed the steep, eroded incline that ran from the narrow beach to the Tower. Her pants were still wet. Her feet made squishy sounds inside the sneakers. She was warm, and not just from the exertion of the climb.

The path threaded its way up between boulders and twisted trees and patches of red wrinkled roses. She paused and looked up at Perth. To her disappointment, he'd put his shirt back on.

Since leaving the beach, he had been quiet, preoccupied. He'd been this way from the moment that he discovered the birthmark on her back.

"Hey, I never thanked you for saving my life," she said, finding herself slightly winded.

He never slowed down or looked back.

"I could have drowned."

Rather than following the path, he took a shortcut by climbing straight up a good-sized boulder with no trouble at all. She struggled, and after a couple of tries she was able to reach the top. She leaned over, her hands on her knees, trying to catch her breath.

"And thank you for fixing me," she said louder. "I still want to know how you did it."

He seemed to be increasing the distance between them.

She straightened and looked out at the cove below. They'd already climbed half way to the top. The flat water reflected the clouds in the distance. At one end of the spit of land that formed the barrier of the salt pond, a channel opened out onto the ocean. Beyond it, the Atlantic roared, its waves crashing onto the rocks and sand.

She couldn't stop marveling what a miracle it was that she'd survived the fall.

"Coming?"

He'd come back for her. He was standing on a rock above. Another shortcut.

"Unlike you, I'm not a mountain goat. I can't climb like that."

"A mountain goat, huh?"

Perth flashed the first real smile she'd seen. When she thought it was impossible for him to become better looking, he proved her wrong. He stretched his hand down.

"I don't trust my arm. What happens if it falls out of its socket?"

He shook his head, the amused expression still there. "Then I'll have to fix you again."

She still hesitated.

"Trust me, Killian."

She took his hand and he easily hauled her up. She rotated her shoulders. All the joints were still intact.

"Tell me something," she asked before he started climbing again. "What were you doing down there? How did you know I fell?"

He pointed to the far end of the salt pond. She saw what looked to be rows of posts just sticking out above the surface off the water. They followed the shoreline. She hadn't noticed them before.

"Aquaculture," he said. "I've been doing course work and internships on it since finishing high school. Part of an undergraduate program through UMass. I was working on the beds when I saw you fall. You weren't exactly quiet on the way down."

"Aquaculture?" She was honestly interested. "That's pretty cool. It's kind of impressive to meet someone who knows what he wants to do with his life."

"Yeah. It's a good backup plan."

Killian turned to him, surprised. "Backup plan? What's at the top of your list?"

He looked at her for a moment before answering. "Getting off this island."

"You're in college. Haven't you technically left?"

"No." He started walking. She fell in step with him.

"What do you mean?"

"The courses, the internships. It's an online program. I live here year round, not on campus."

"But you have *left* the island." She had to make sure.

"Only day trips to the mainland."

Killian remembered how isolated she'd felt at times going to school in Vermont. She couldn't imagine being stuck there after high school. "But why not longer? What's stopping you from doing what you want to do?"

"Family. Responsibility. Walt wouldn't be able to manage without me." He picked up the pace.

Killian tried to imagine what was worse. Her situation with a dad who'd been more than happy to cut the ties...or his with a father who was completely dependent on him. Perth might be stuck here indefinitely.

"How about you?" he asked. "Hannah said you're done with high school. Do you know what you want to do?"

"I should, I guess."

"But you don't?"

It was difficult to admit that she'd been given plenty of opportunities to find out what she wanted. A good school. A first-class education. When it came to actually making decisions about applying to colleges, though, she hadn't done anything.

"I've had some issues."

"Family trouble?"

She looked at him, surprised.

"Hannah mentioned that you lost your mother to cancer and your father married again."

Killian shrugged. "It's been four years."

It may have been four years, but she wasn't past it. She was still angry at her mother for dying and leaving her alone. Angry at her father for marrying again and starting a new family that didn't include her.

"Time isn't always a healer. It can't be too easy."

"It's not."

There was a cloud in front of her that she couldn't see beyond. She didn't know where she belonged or where she was going.

"But I have nobody to blame but myself for not being able to decide what I'm going to do with my life."

Perth brushed the back of his hand against hers. She appreciated the gesture and looked up toward the Tower. The bottom line was that his problems were real. Hers were just emotional.

They continued up the hill. Killian noticed that Perth was going slower, making sure she was keeping up.

She knew her imagination was working overtime, but she couldn't help herself. It might actually be a bright spot in her life if she and Perth sort of became friends. At least while she was on the island. She wasn't ridiculous enough to think there could be anything romantic between them. He was way too hot to be interested in her that way. But it might be cool just to have a friend she could hang out with.

Maybe Hannah hadn't been so totally out there with her plotting.

At the top Killian turned and looked up the grassy knoll that led out to the Tower.

"No sign of him," she said.

"Come on. We'll get your backpack."

Approaching the Tower from this angle, Killian could see a side of the building she hadn't seen before, and another doorway. This one was wide open. They made their way around to the other side, but there was no sign of her pack.

"It was right here," she said, pointing to the ground near the boarded-up entrance. "If that guy thinks he can just let someone fall off a cliff and then take their pack—"

"Let's look inside."

As Perth led her around the Tower, Killian kept looking for Lynx, half-expecting the old man to suddenly materialize as he seemed to do before.

Three steps carved out of the rock led down to the open door, and Perth ducked his head as he went in. Following him, Killian stayed close, squinting as her eyes adjusted to the darkness inside.

The floor was made of large paving stones, with bits of broken glass visible in the cracks in between. Two battered, rusted tables sat against one wall. Killian half expected to see beer cans and bottles littering the place. Perth was standing by a burned out fire, holding her backpack.

"This it?" he asked.

"Great!" she said, relieved.

Taking it from him, she pulled out her tee-shirt and put it on.

"Guess my stuff didn't match Lynx's wardrobe," she joked.

Perth was staring at the cold ashes of the fire. She followed his gaze as he looked up at the blackened wood beams above them.

"Somebody trying to burn the place down?"

"Unintentionally, I suppose," he responded vaguely.

Looking back at her, he gestured toward a set of stone stairs that ran upward along the curved wall. At the top, she could see an opening leading to the upper floor.

"Come on, I want to show you something."

Killian followed him up the steps, staying close to the wall. She didn't need two falls in one day.

The room above was empty, but three windows let in plenty of light. Fingers of sea breeze threaded through Killian's hair and caressed her face. She took a deep breath. Calm seeped into her bones. A feeling of...confidence...unlike any she'd ever felt before. Standing in the center of the room, she turned around, looking out each window.

"I like this place," she said quietly.

A set of stairs—identical to the ones below—led up to the ramparts. Through the opening in the beams above, she could see blue sky.

"Are we going up?"

"If you want to," he said. "But this is what I wanted you to see."

Killian looked around her, perplexed.

Perth pointed to the floor. "This."

The Tower walls formed a perfect circle, but the floor beams had been arranged to create a specific design. The shape of a five-pointed star.

She was standing at the center of a pentagram.

"It matches the mark on your back."

Killian looked from the patterned floor to Perth's face.

His eyes were as cold as a winter sea.

CHAPTER 8

Devil worshippers, bloody cult rituals, aliens stealing earth babies to do experiments. Oh yeah, and fallen angels who looked suspiciously like Perth, intent on seducing seventeen-year-old high school students and 'fixing' them.

What a night. Killian lay awake for the longest time. She couldn't go to sleep with lightning flashing right outside her window. Explosions of thunder shook the house. The wind howled. With the pillow pulled over her face, Killian finally drifted off into a fitful sleep. Bits of nightmares, like flashing shards of glass, seemed to reflect fragments of hallucination and reality. She floated back and forth endlessly in that restless state, all the while trying to hang on to the fallen angel part of her dreams.

Voices. What were the voices in her head?

...capsized...
...called in...
...find Perth...
...harbor...
...everyone...

Suddenly, the urgent sound of sirens overwhelmed all other noise, drowning out the voices in her dream. Killian opened her eyes. It was no dream.

Startled, she sat up in bed. It was still dark. She looked at the sheets of gale-driven rain slapping against the window. She glanced at the bedside clock. 2:18.

The sirens were still going.

Killian's days of dorm life rushed back. Fire alarms. Tornado warnings. Lightning hitting the school science building. Some bored teenager pulling the lever as a prank. She looked around the room again. Everything came into focus. Cuttylea Island. Hannah's cottage.

She hurried into some clothes. The storm pounded the windows and walls. On the way out of her room, Killian grabbed her father's windbreaker.

The door to Hannah's bedroom was open. The light was on, but there was no sign of her aunt. Killian hurried downstairs. As she entered the kitchen, the screen door banged hard against its frame. Rain was pushing under the kitchen door, seeping into the doormat.

Hannah must have left the house in a hurry, Killian thought.

Pulling on the windbreaker, she stepped into her damp sneakers and went out. At the paved road, she shielded her eyes and peered down the hill toward the waterfront. A crowd had gathered beneath the lights at the dock.

When she was halfway down the hill, the blaring sirens suddenly stopped. As she approached, everyone seemed to be talking at once.

"…only two of them."

"…washed over the side."

"…he's dead."

"…she isn't breathing."

"…Perth…"

It looked to Killian as if everyone on the island had gathered by the docks and the adjacent beach area. At the center, people were bent over two bodies.

Help me.

The protected water of the inner harbor wasn't being spared by the gusting wind and rain. The masts of sailboats rocked violently. Waves banged at their hulls, and the clanging of bells added to the noise. Two tall boys in yellow rain slickers were hauling a capsized dingy out of the water. She looked around for Perth, but she couldn't see him.

I need you.

She couldn't tell who was calling out. The voice could have belonged to any number of people on the dock.

I know you can hear me. You are the only one. Help me.

Killian pushed through the crowd toward the voice. She recognized Thomas Eliot. The old man was dropping a tarp over the body of a man lying on the dock.

"Killian."

She was relieved to hear Hannah's voice. Turning, she saw her aunt kneeling beside a second body.

"What are you doing down here?"

Killian knelt beside her aunt and stared down at the young woman lying on the dock. The gray mask of death stretched across her face.

"What happened?"

"Mainlanders. Their boat must have gone down somewhere outside the breakwater." Hannah nodded toward the other victim. "His foot was tangled in a rope dragging behind the dingy. She had a pulse when we dragged her out of the water, but now..." She shook her head.

Help me.

Killian started. The woman was staring at her. Killian reached out and took her hand. Icy fingers sat stiffly in her grip. Hannah was saying something about the storm. Others were shouting directions. There was too much noise in her head.

My boys.

"She's alive," Killian gasped. "A doctor. She needs a doctor."

"The Coast Guard is on the way. They're sending a chopper," someone said over her shoulder.

My two boys. In the cabin of the boat.

Hannah was leaning close to her, speaking over the storm and the other voices. "It's too late. She's gone."

As Killian turned to answer, a feeling of calm washed over her. Suddenly, she sensed that Perth was near. She saw him coming down the beach. He was wearing only shorts and looking like he'd just stepped out of the water.

Not enough time. Help them.

Killian looked back down into the woman's face.

Squibnocket. On the rocks. Our sailboat. Her voice was getting weaker. *Save my boys.*

"Her two sons. We have to save them." Killian said aloud. "Squibnocket. On the rocks. They're still on the boat."

The crowd stared. The only one to react immediately was Perth. He ran down the dock. A shaft of lightning ripped through the sky beyond the breakwater, illuminating the harbor just as he dove into the black water and disappeared.

When she looked back down at the woman, the eyes in the gray face were closed.

Hannah gestured toward tufts of sea grass and sand to the left of the golf cart.

"Squibnocket."

Killian shielded her eyes against the driving rain and tried to see where her aunt was pointing. Not far off, waves crashed over the rocky ledge of shoreline. The salt spray on the wind stung her face. She couldn't see anything out on the water.

Her aunt's old cart could not keep up with the island's utility truck. By the time they reached the narrow point of land, a half dozen men and women had unloaded a launch. They were dragging it into the water.

As the two made their way across the sand, Killian saw the bow of the launch suddenly lift high in the air, threatening to topple over onto the islanders. The boat teetered a moment and then slammed back down.

Lightning raked across the sky, followed by deafening thunder.

"It's still on the reef," Hannah said.

Killian peered out into the storm. High waves were battering the white hull of the stranded boat.

The launch's engine roared to life as a series of lightning flashes lit up the sky.

"Look!" Hannah pulled at her sleeve.

But Killian had already seen him. Perth was pulling himself up onto the overturned sailboat. Then, as the flash of light disappeared, a massive wave struck the boat, washing over him.

The next flash showed that the reef was clear. The sailboat was gone.

The sea and sky were black, and Killian strained for a glimpse of anything.

Suddenly, a shout went up as a figure rose from the surf and climbed onto the rocky ledge.

It was Perth, with one boy on his back and another in his arms.

CHAPTER 9

"I know I told Hannah that things might be slow this week, but we've had a little change in plans."

"That's no problem," Killian murmured, stifling a sleepy yawn.

She looked down at the list of jobs that Elena Adams, the innkeeper, had put together for her.

"Now, I don't want you to get scared and quit on me," Elena said quickly, using a flour-covered hand to push a wisp of graying hair off her forehead. She leaned on the bread board and took a deep breath.

One floor-mounted, industrial-sized mixer by the kitchen island. Numerous bowls so big you could wash a baby in them. Pan after pan of dough already shaped and covered with towels. A 30-pound sack of flour and jars of spices on every counter. Killian glanced at the door of a walk-in cooler. She guessed there would be a few loaves of bread going in there today. A fat, striped gray cat sat curled up on top of a refrigerator, watching the activity without interest.

Clearly, Elena had been at her baking for quite a while already. Most likely, from the time she'd returned after the rescue of those two boys last night. It was now 9:00 a.m.

"You're the first to get out here to the island. I have three other girls who will arrive tomorrow. They'll be working with you on different shifts. This 'To Do' list is ongoing stuff. The four of you need to take care of these jobs every day for the whole summer."

"This is all cool. Where do you want me to start?"

Killian was exhausted. She'd been so tempted this morning to walk in here and make some excuse and try to get the rest of the day off. But she couldn't do it when she saw Elena literally up to her elbows in flour.

"I like you already." The innkeeper smiled. "And I'm glad you came in with your work clothes on. Getting the inn ready for the summer season is a dirty job."

Killian looked down at the white tee-shirt and jean shorts she was wearing. They were actually good clothes.

"Why don't you take the sheets and towels out of the dryer in there and fold them while I finish this batch. Then I'll give you a twenty-five cent tour of the place before getting you started on what I had in mind."

The washer and dryer were in a combination pantry and laundry room off the kitchen. Killian's gaze was drawn to a basket of colored sea glass sitting on a shelf. Every piece was different, polished smooth by countless tides.

"These are pretty," she said.

"I think so, too. I pick them up when I see them." Elena smiled. "You'll find bowls of them all over the inn. I didn't pick any up last night. We were a little busy, weren't we?"

Before leaving the cottage this morning, Killian asked Hannah about what was going to become of the two rescued boys. In a way, she almost hoped last night had been a dream. But it wasn't. Hannah said the children had already been taken back to the mainland by the Coast Guard.

Losing parents was a heartbreak. Killian knew that. She and Perth had each lost a mother, and they continued to suffer from it.

Perth. She took an armful of linen out of the dryer and dumped it on the folding table. They hadn't spoken after the rescue of those boys. His attempts at being a conversationalist had ended yesterday afternoon.

Standing in the circular Tower room, she asked him why that pentagram was built into the floor. He just shrugged, saying he didn't know anything about it. After that, he'd taken Killian as far as the town dump, where they'd met up with an ancient islander hauling trash in the back of an equally ancient truck. There'd been no sign of Lynx, and Perth said he had to get back to work on the beds at the pond. Killian hitched a ride back to the village in the truck.

Back at the cottage, Killian hoped her aunt could explain away some of the strange happenings of the day. But Hannah came home late in the afternoon with two other people who stayed for dinner—Daniel Sawyer, the man of many hats, and his wife. The guests sat around until the winds began to pick up, and Killian's aunt went up to bed minutes after they'd left. And then the storm had really let loose.

Killian finished folding the sheets and towels.

"Perfect timing," the innkeeper said, coming into the laundry room. "Let me show you around."

Killian followed her new boss. They took the back stairs to the second floor.

"I run this place as a bed-and-breakfast from mid-June to Labor Day. I rely on the summer income to pay for the upkeep of the inn and my year-round living expenses."

Killian wondered about Elena's age. She had salt-and-pepper hair pulled back into a ponytail. Killian hadn't seen kids around the house, but she decided if Elena had any, they would be older. There was no wedding ring on her finger.

"Have you lived on the island all your life?"

"Most of it, anyway."

"Were you here twenty...twenty-five years ago?" Killian asked.

"I sure was," Elena answered as they reached the second floor.

"Do you remember my mother? She used to summer here with Hannah."

"I remember Ama. She worked for me here at the inn. She did exactly what you'll be doing this summer."

"You must have been pretty young then, yourself."

The innkeeper smiled and led Killian from room to room.

"I have twelve guest rooms on the second and third floor of this building. And the two cottages—a one bedroom and a two bedroom—are just down the hill from the inn."

They reached the end of the hall.

"I expect you and the other girls..." Elena continued.

She is here.

I want to see her.

You will, in time.

No. I want to meet her now.

You'll have to wait.

I can't. And I don't like the way the rest of you—

"Are you coming?" Elena's voice brought Killian back to reality.

She found herself standing by a partly open door. The innkeeper had walked past it on the way to the stairs leading to the third floor. Instead of the usual brass number, a blue ceramic plate with a pentagram painted on it hung on the door. The fat gray cat came down the hall and sat, tail twitching.

"Won't I be taking care of this room, too? Shouldn't I see it?"

"No. That's not one of the guest rooms."

"Who lives there?"

"Family." Elena went up the stairs.

Killian followed, but behind her she saw the door open a little wider. When she looked back, she saw the cat disappear into the room.

"Is that where you live?"

"No, I have an apartment on the first floor, at the back of the house."

"And who in your family lives there?"

"My mother and an aunt." Elena reached the third floor landing. She waited for Killian to join her. "You don't have to worry about their rooms. Mine, either. You'll have plenty to do with the guest rooms and serving times. We advertise bed-and-breakfast, but in reality we serve three meals a day to our guests. It's not like there are any other restaurants on the island people can go to. And with the exception of the people in the cottages, our guests need a place to eat."

The third-floor ceilings were lower and the rooms much smaller. Gables and dormers with windows created a lot of cozy nooks in the rooms. It was all very nice, she thought, and the job would certainly keep her busy. She would be housekeeper, waitress, kitchen help, gofer, and whatever else Elena needed her to be. The good news was that she got paid by the hour, and anything over forty hours would be overtime.

Downstairs, Elena took an oversized tee-shirt off a peg in the back hallway and handed it to her before they went out to see the cottages. "You'll need this."

Killian looked at the stains on the shirt. "I'll be doing some painting today?"

Elena nodded. "I mentioned we had a last-minute change of plans."

A neatly designed gravel path curved down a grassy hill to two quaint cottages nestled some fifty feet apart.

"Yesterday, I had a call from the Department of Energy and Environmental Affairs in Boston. They're sending a team of researchers to the island and want to rent the cottages for the whole season. They're arriving in two days."

"What are they researching?"

"Wind power. The possibility of putting wind farms in the ocean near Cuttylea Island and sending the energy back to the mainland."

Killian gazed out at the uninterrupted view of blue water straight ahead. "The islanders have no problem with it?"

Elena shrugged. "If everything works out, they'll put up the wind turbines some three miles off the coast. The folks who live here year round will get free utilities and a small monthly income from the power company."

Less than two days on the island, and Killian had walked by every house. If the inside of Hannah's cottage was a fair example; people lived comfortably but frugally here. No mini-mansions. No show of lavish living on the part of the locals. She guessed the extra income would be welcome.

"They're arriving on Sunday? That's three days before you're officially open."

"You got it. My bigger problem is that both cottages are already booked for half the weeks of the summer."

"How flexible are they?"

"Not at all. And you don't say 'no' to people from the State. It's hard to pass up a one hundred percent booking for the season."

At the first cottage, the front door was open. Drop cloths were spread from the stairs into the front room. The smell of fresh paint wafted out. Someone inside was already at work.

"I'm trying to make my phone calls today and move whatever cottage reservations I can to the main house. In the meantime, I want you to help finish the painting by tomorrow."

Painting was art to Killian. She'd never painted walls. Still, she knew she could handle it. "Okay, where do I start?"

"In this cottage."

Killian's stomach tightened as Perth came out of one of the bedrooms, and it struck her that her body got a mind of its own whenever he showed up. And when he wasn't around, she couldn't shake him—awake or asleep.

"Perth will tell you what to do."

CHAPTER 10

No small talk. No discussion of weird old Lynx or her fall off the cliff. No mention of the Tower. No chance to even bring up what Perth had done last night. They might as well have been total strangers.

"Paint, stepladders, drop cloths, brushes, scrapers, sandpaper. Rubber gloves in that bag if you want to use them. Make sure you scrape off the old loose paint and wipe the surface clean before you put on new paint. And try not to spatter the porch or spill anything on the grass by the railing."

He was painting the walls inside the two-bedroom cottage and told her she was to start with the outside trim of the other one. They couldn't even work on the same building together.

Elena had gone back to the house. Perth continued on with his instructions. It was impossible not to be affected by the coldness he was treating her with. The bossy tone. She was clearly an intruder in his space. He didn't want her even in the same building.

Fine, she thought. If that's the way he wants it.

"Yell if you need anything," he said, making no eye-contact.

Disappointed, Killian watched him walk away and wondered what was behind the change. This was the same attitude he'd laid on her after they left the Tower yesterday afternoon.

"And they say girls are moody," she grumbled under her breath.

She dragged all the supplies to a grassy area by the covered cottage porch. She knew she was totally sleep-deprived. Not the best time to dwell on Perth and his attitude.

Killian still couldn't get her iPod working, but she was getting paid to do a job, so she might as well get to it. Looking at her reflection in the window, she pulled her dark hair into a tight ponytail. The tee-shirt Elena had given her reached mid-thigh. She pulled it over her other clothes and rolled up the

"Seriously, how did you do it?" Josh persisted.

"Uh, I have work to do." She ran the brush over the woodwork. It had taken her four years to come to terms with always being an outsider. She wasn't going to let people think she was a freak.

Josh wasn't giving up. "Come on. It's pretty cool."

"Let it go," Eric snapped at his friend. He smiled. "So where are you staying?"

Killian glanced at the two staring up at her and wondered if Elena was paying them by the hour. They weren't going anywhere. It was time to move the ladder.

"I arrived two days ago. I'm staying with family," she said, shifting the paint and brush to one hand and backing down the steps. "Listen, no Twenty Questions right now. Elena is panicky enough about getting ready without us slowing things down."

She started to slide the ladder across the porch. Both of them jumped to do it for her.

"You probably already figured out that not much happens in this place," Eric said.

"So the summer help hang out together," Josh added with a hint of suggestion.

"We make our own party."

"That's the only way to get through."

"We hang at night out on the Point," Eric told her. "By the lighthouse."

Between two muscular guys and the ladder, it was way too crowded on the porch. She went down the steps onto the grass.

"Why don't you come out tonight?" he continued.

"I was told most of the summer people aren't here, yet," Killian replied.

"Hey, we have three of us. That's enough for a party," Josh said with a grin.

Killian remembered their words before they'd reached her. Fresh meat. Shotgun. She might be boyfriend-deprived, but she wasn't stupid.

"We'll have a good time," Josh persisted.

"I have to keep going before my brush dries," Killian said quietly.

"Exactly! Seize the day!"

"Never mind him." Eric stepped down to join her on the grass. "After you get out of work, maybe we can meet up at the pier. Last night, the ice cream shack was already open, and they serve hot dogs and hamburgers. It's just nice to—"

"Killian."

She didn't have to turn around to recognize Perth's voice. The tone was way too sharp. She looked up at Eric. "You were saying?"

"How about if we meet up after work by the pier? Say…sixish?"

"Killian, I've been calling you."

"I heard you," she said, keeping her temper in check.

"Josh. Eric," Perth said, greeting them shortly before turning to her. "I'm ready for you to start on the trim at the other cottage."

"You work for him?" Eric wanted to know.

"Not *for* me," Perth said. "*With* me."

The two young men were standing eye-to-eye. Same size, same build. Neither moved. It was like watching a nature show with two lions about to fight over a leg of gazelle. Their dislike for each other was too evident. Killian wondered about the history between these two. There had to be something.

"Let's go, youngsters," she blurted out like a camp counselor. "We've got cottages to paint, roofs to fix, a business to get up and running."

Killian didn't wait for them to respond, but grabbed the brush and paint can and started for the other cottage. Half a dozen steps away, she found Perth walking back with her.

"So, what about tonight at 6:00?" Eric called out from behind.

Killian felt Perth's body tense up as she stopped and looked back.

"Maybe," she said, turning and walking ahead of Perth to the cottage.

CHAPTER 11

"Are you schizo?"

"Excuse me?" Perth straightened up after dropping the ladder on the grass next to the porch steps.

The larger cottage was totally painted. They were done with the outside trim and ceiling work on the second building. The brushes were washed and hung to dry. All other supplies had been neatly stacked in the corner of the living room. They'd worked most of the afternoon close together, and he'd not once snapped her head off or pulled his 'I-am-too-cool-and-collected-to-talk-with-hired-help' routine. Actually, he'd been darn pleasant since Eric and Josh finished on the roof and went back up to the inn.

"I said, are you schizo?" she said, looking innocently at him. "Either one of you can answer."

"No," he said, the hint of smile creasing the corners of his green eyes.

"Are you sure?" she asked as they started up the path toward the main house.

Their shoulders bumped as they walked. She had sunburn on her upper-arms, and her skin sizzled as it came in contact with his.

"Do you think I'm schizoid?"

Killian stole a glance at his handsome face and tried to calm the butterflies ravaging her insides.

"Look at the way you act. You've been short, rude, mean...*and* you've been considerate, kind, and almost charming to me. And all in the course of a single day."

"Almost charming? Hold it." He stopped her and reached over to wipe a smudge on her nose. "You missed a spot of paint."

Her heart kicked into sprint mode. "Okay, I overstated that. Pleasant. You were pleasant."

"Better. I have a rep to protect."

At the inn, they poked their heads into the kitchen. Elena was on the phone. She waved and mouthed that she'd see them tomorrow. Killian hung the painting shirt on a peg as they went out.

"Five of six," Perth said when they reached the road. Just like that, the edge in his voice was back.

She looked up at him, amazed. "There we go again. Grizzly Adams returns."

"I'm just mentioning the time." He pointed down the street. "That's the way to the pier. I believe that's where the party starts."

"Did I ask you for the time or for directions?" She crossed her arms and glared up into his face. "Are you my social secretary?"

No answer. He started walking up the road. She fell in beside him.

"I'm not a shrink. But something is definitely going on with you."

"Really? *I* didn't say I was going to meet them at the pier."

"Neither did I. I said *maybe*. Maybe is only a maybe. Nothing more."

Killian didn't know where he was heading, but it didn't matter. She just knew she wasn't going to party with two boys she didn't know.

The golden rays of the descending sun lit up the road and trees and beach grass. Their shadows stretched out in front of them as they walked on in silence.

This was where she wanted to be. With Perth. She'd enjoyed the hours that they'd worked side-by-side today. Camaraderie was not a normal feeling for her. In spite of his mood shifts, what she was feeling when she was with him was very cool.

"I'm not schizoid, exactly," he said, breaking the silence. "But when it comes to trusting certain people, I choose to be...well, bipolar."

"Choose to be? I don't think that's how our psyche works," she told him. "Wait! What 'certain' people?"

He turned his gaze on her, and for a second or two, Killian forgot to breathe as he studied her face, looking into her eyes.

"What are you doing here, Killian?"

His question startled her. "Here? Right now?"

"What's your connection to Cuttylea Island?"

They'd stopped at the top of a hill. The guarded expression was back in his face.

"I'm out here for a job," she said. "Same as other people who come here in the summer."

"But you're not *like* any of them. And I'm not talking about the way you look or talk or even act. I could name a dozen ways that the summer crowd all are pretty much the same, but you're not like them."

The words could have been meant as a compliment, but his tone killed it. Killian felt a chill crawl in and grab her gut with an icy hand. Something hurt in the way he said the words and she stepped back. But before she could walk away, his hand darted out. He took hold of her arm.

"I don't trust you, either," she snapped, trying to shake off his hand. "I don't know you. But I'm civil enough that I don't make stupid accusations over nothing. I have to get back to Hannah."

"That's not what I'm saying." He shook his head.

"I have to get home."

"Wait. I want to show you something."

"No."

"Please," he said, much gentler, his thumb caressing the skin on her arm before releasing her. "You need to see this."

Killian should have walked away, but she couldn't. Already, an invisible tie was connecting them.

"This is the oldest house on the island."

Perth pushed open an iron gate that creaked noisily. He led her into a shadowy, overgrown garden. Roses and vines had long ago grown into a complete tangle. Weeds had taken over flowerbeds. Clearly, no one had been taking care of the garden for quite some time. A chill ran down her spine.

"Does anyone live here?"

"Yeah, an old couple. I don't think they get out much."

Killian looked up at the house. It was dark and as neglected as the garden. There was no sign of life.

"Should we be in here?" She was not feeling good about this.

He shrugged and walked toward what must have been an herb garden at one time. Now it was just a mess.

"Look at this."

Perth climbed into the center of it. A circular space was covered only by some spreading herb. He got down on one knee and pushed aside the ground covering plant. The sweet, tangy smell filled Killian's senses. She crouched down beside him.

Beneath the plants was a slab. She stared for a moment in disbelief at the large pentagram that had been carved into the stone. No writing, only the sign.

"You saw the one in the Tower."

And she'd seen it back at the inn.

"What?" She stood up.

"Just a coincidence that there's another pentagram here? In a garden of the oldest house on the island?" He didn't wait for her to respond. "And this isn't the only one."

"So?"

"Every house on Cuttylea has this mark. Either inside or outside. Every one."

"Have you ever been to Nantucket or Newport? There must be ten thousand pineapples engraved on stones and signs and on flags on houses and…they're everywhere!"

"Yeah, but you don't have the mark of a pineapple on your back."

She stood up. "I don't know what you're saying here, but you're weirding me out. I have to get home to Hannah."

"Okay. Let's go. But there's one more thing I want to show you on the way."

It was only a few minutes later, but the sun was hanging just above the western horizon when Perth turned into a walled-in cemetery next to the road. Killian could see the roof of Hannah's house from the entrance.

"A graveyard?"

"It'll just take a minute."

"Let me guess. Pentagrams on the gravestones?"

Perth pointed past the rows of weathered headstones. One section of the cemetery was walled off from the rest. It was on a gentle slope that faced the ocean. Killian followed him through a narrow opening in the wall.

Some of the dozen or so graves looked to have been there for quite a while. She gazed at the one that appeared to be the oldest. The carving was nearly eroded away, but she could read one of the dates.

"1642."

"Look at the name," Perth said. "Look at them all."

Killian's blood ran cold as she went from one grave to the next. The dates were getting closer to the present. They were all women. A pentagram was carved into every stone. And every one had the same first or middle name.

Ama.

The last grave was only four years old, and the name on the headstone was 'Ama Tanith Fitch'.

Killian's mother.

CHAPTER 12

"Why didn't you tell me she was buried here?"

"It's been two days, sweetheart," Hannah said gently, following Killian into the living room. "You only arrived two days ago. And we haven't had too many moments alone together. I was going to take you over there and show you the grave myself. On your first day off."

A lacy antique spread covered the back of the sofa, and Killian sank down on the edge of it, dropping her head into her hands.

The whole thing was unbelievable. Seeing her mother's name on the gravestone, she'd simply stared at it, totally stunned. Her first thought was that the grave had to be someone else's. But the name and the dates matched perfectly. Then panic had gripped her. She didn't know what happened to Perth. She just remembered pushing by him and running all the way to Hannah's cottage.

Killian glanced up as Hannah sat down on a rocking chair across the room.

"I was told my mother was cremated."

"Your father didn't want to bring you back here. He arranged for a beautiful funeral and said his goodbyes. What happened to Ama's body after that was really not important to him."

Killian remembered her mother's casket at the back of the church. That was the last time she'd seen it. A couple of years later, she asked her father what he'd done with the ashes. He told her he'd scattered them on Long Island Sound. It was what Ama wanted, he said.

He lied.

"And you brought her back here. Why?"

"It's the family plot. That's where her mother and grandmother are buried."

She took in the old woman's sincere expression. "Why didn't you bring me back with you? At least, for the burial."

"I wanted to, but your father wouldn't allow it. Rick wanted closure for both of you, and he felt the church service in Connecticut would be enough."

"You could have asked me, anyway. I'm her *daughter*."

"You were thirteen. I wasn't about to question Rick's decision, not after what the two of you had just gone through."

Killian remembered all the times when she'd struggled to hold on to her mother's memory. She'd searched out photos, stories from people Ama knew, anything. How many times had she wished there was a grave that she could go to? A place where she could feel closer to her.

"Does he ever come out here and visit her grave?"

"No. But I don't blame him. He has his new wife and children to consider."

Angry now, Killian jumped to her feet. *Consider?* She'd witnessed it firsthand. Her father pretended Ama never lived.

"This isn't closure. This is erasing the woman you supposedly loved from your memory."

"You can't live Rick's life, honey," Hannah told her.

"I don't want to live his life. I only want him to acknowledge that my mother existed!" That *I* exist, she silently finished.

"There's no point to all this anger, Killian. Your father...and the rest of us...we all do the best we can with the lives we're given. Right now, you're at a stage in life where you're carving out your own path. Making your own decisions. Planning your own future. I loved your mother, but that's only a body lying in that grave. A pile of bones. You're keeping her memory alive here." She pointed at her heart. "And that's all that matters."

Killian rubbed her temples. She wanted to accept Hannah's words. She'd hoped to find memories of her mother on Cuttylea. Now she knew there were plenty.

"I know it's too late today, but I want to go back there. To the cemetery. With you."

"We can go there any time you like. Just tell me when and we'll do it."

Killian nodded.

Hannah stood up and walked toward the kitchen. "Dinner is pretty much ready. I made fish chowder, and the clam fritters will only take a few minutes to fry up."

"Thanks." It was difficult to focus on mundane things like food right now when there were so many questions bombarding her mind.

Hannah disappeared into the kitchen.

Killian stood up and walked to the kitchen door, watching her aunt turn the gas on under a deep, cast iron frying pan.

"That family plot. Why are there only women buried there?"

Hannah made a production of stirring the chowder before looking at her. "You know, I never really thought about it. But I guess…men went to sea. They were always sailors or fishermen or whalers. Later on, soldiers. Women stayed here and kept the home fires burning. That would be my guess."

Killian couldn't wait to go back there. She wanted to read every headstone. She wanted to know everything about these women who were her family. Hannah was the only relative on her mother's side that she'd ever known.

"And the name 'Ama'. Every one of those women had that name as their first name or their middle name. Same as me. Why?"

This time Hannah's gaze didn't waver. "That's tradition. Your mother must have explained the significance of it."

"She said we have Cherokee blood." Killian looked into Hannah's blue eyes behind the thick lenses of her glasses. So unlike the dark eyes of her mother. So unlike Killian's. "Ama is a Cherokee name."

"And do you know what 'Ama' means?"

"Water."

"It's a great honor to carry that name. You have to be born to it." Hannah turned her attention back to the stove. "These fritters will be on the table in fifteen. They're best when they're hot."

Limits exist to be pushed. In high school, Killian assumed four miles was her limit for running. Then, senior year, she'd done fifteen miles in a breast cancer fundraiser. The same thing was true when her father and his new wife decided that the limit on moping around after graduation was only a day or two. She'd proven them wrong. Killian stayed clear of their family activities until leaving for Cuttylea Island.

Unfortunately, the same thing was happening here with sleeping. There was no limit on how little sleep she got. She no longer needed it, apparently.

She moved her pillow so she could see the bright white moon rising over the harbor. Through the open window came the gentle rustle of leaves, the song of crickets, the surge and slap of waves on a not too distant beach.

Tonight, sounds weren't to blame for Killian's inability to sleep. Her mind was cranking with thoughts and memories.

Hannah's light had gone off a couple of hours ago. Killian had turned hers off, too, after finishing a short story. It was in a book one of her English teachers had given her as a graduation gift. There was nothing else to do. No listening to her iPod. No watching movies or television. No sending texts or calling anyone or getting on Facebook and creeping on her classmates. Still, Killian wasn't bored. She was happy to lie here and inhale the smells and listen to the sounds of the island. To watch the moon rise.

A screen door slammed not far away. She heard the hollow sound of wheels rolling on a wooden platform. Killian decided the noise was coming from Perth's house. His father Walt was going down the ramp on his wheelchair. She wondered if Perth was home or if he was out on one of his nightly swims to England and back.

A metallic sounding crash, followed by profuse cursing, caused Killian to jump out of bed. She leaned out the window. She could just make out the wheelchair flipped on its side, the spinning spokes reflecting the moonlight. A dark shape was struggling in the grass next to it.

Tugging on shorts and a sweatshirt, Killian went quickly down the stairs and out the kitchen door.

"You okay?" she called from the safety of Hannah's garden.

"Just dandy," a gruff voice bellowed.

The chair was still on its side. Beyond it, Perth's father was struggling. She walked toward him. "Do you need help?"

"No."

"Should I get Hannah?"

"Damn it, no! I'm fine."

She glanced toward the house. There was no sign of Perth. Walt was now sitting, but the chair was out of his reach. She walked toward it.

"Go away," he growled, this time half-heartedly.

Killian reached the chair and pulled it upright. The wheels hit the ground with a ringing sound.

Walt peered at her in the dark. "You don't listen too well, do you?"

"No," she replied, pushing the chair closer to him. "Hi, I'm Killian."

"You don't say."

"Hannah's grandniece."

"I know," he said in an exasperated tone, reaching for the arm of the wheelchair.

Killian moved beside him and unconsciously touched his elbow, wondering how she could help him. "Are you hurt?"

"No," he grumbled. "Why don't you go back to whatever hole you popped out of?"

"I will as soon as you're back in your chair."

For the first time, he stopped muttering and really looked at her. Compared to a lot of the locals she'd met, Walt was younger. Killian guessed he was about the same age as her father. But he looked thin, frail. He was small built to begin with, and he had none of his son's vitality. She also decided Perth had to get his good looks from his mother.

"What are you doing out here in the middle of the night?" he asked.

"Helping a grouchy neighbor."

He shook his head and reached up a hand toward her. She took it. His grip was surprisingly strong, and after a couple of tries he was back in the wheelchair.

Killian waited until she was sure he could maneuver on his own on the grass.

"You're dismissed," he ordered.

"Are you sure that's all the excitement you can muster for tonight?" she asked.

"A regular comedian," he muttered, looking around him on the ground. Spotting a small cellophane wrapped box near some long grass, he pointed to it. "Be useful. Get that for me."

Killian picked it up and handed it to him. Cigars.

He took one out and pulled a lighter from his pocket. He offered her one. "You smoke?"

She smiled in the darkness. "No. I should be getting back."

"Now you're in a hurry."

He lit the cigar and puffed at it until the end of it was glowing red. The smell wafted toward her, triggering some memory from her childhood. She couldn't put her finger on it. He pointed to the flat top of a rock pushing up through the beach grass.

"I saved the nicest seat in the house for you," he said, blowing smoke into the air.

So much about Perth was a mystery, and Killian couldn't help but be curious about the man who'd raised him. She sat on the rock. Walt smoked in silence for a minute or so.

"Killian." He tested her name on his tongue. "I'm surprised. But I like you."

"Surprised?"

"Okay, shocked," he replied. "I hear you were involved with the rescue of those boys. That's pretty impressive."

She understood where Perth learned his slick moves. Insult them and compliment them in the same breath.

"I didn't do anything. It was Perth who saved them. He's quite a swimmer."

"Yeah, he's something," Walt said. The gruffness in his voice couldn't hide the note of pride. "Actually, he's the reason why I'm out here."

"What do you mean?"

"He doesn't want me smoking in the house. Figures I'll smoke less if I have to come outside." Walt chuckled wryly, holding up his cigar. "As if this thing is going to kill me."

"Smoking isn't too good for your health."

"Hell, if it's time to punch my ticket, then let's do it. I'm ready to go, any time." He contemplated the glowing end of the stogie. "That's the problem with too many people; they just hang around too long. You see this cigar?"

"I do," she said.

"When I lit it, this thing was exactly four inches long. Now I can enjoy every bit of it, or I can spend my time worrying about how I'm going to stretch it out. That make any sense to you?"

"Are you promoting cigar smoking to a teenager?"

"I'm promoting something, but damned if I know what," he replied with a chuckle.

He was twisted, she thought, different from most adults she knew. She liked him.

"Well, whatever it is, you're a terrible salesman."

"Thank you. You're pretty rotten rescue worker yourself."

"You'll never win anything at the Paralympics."

"At least, I won't drown in the fifty-meter freestyle...or in the kiddie pool."

"Good one." Killian laughed, stealing a glance toward the harbor. Walt had, no doubt, heard from Perth that she couldn't swim. The end of the cigar glowed as he puffed on it, lighting up his face. He seemed at ease. Relaxed.

"The first morning I was here, I saw you and the other islanders coming from the woods." Killian decided she might as well ask. She already had a feeling Walt was not one to evade a question. "Where were you all coming from?"

"The Tower."

"But that's so far away."

"Not if you know the shortcut."

"Why would everyone go there?"

He looked steadily at her in the dark for a moment. "To talk about you."

Now Killian didn't know if he was teasing her or telling the truth. He'd already revealed more than Hannah had admitted.

"Why would—?"

She heard footsteps and turned her attention toward the road. Neither said anything more, and in a moment Perth emerged like a shadow from the darkness.

"What's going on?" he asked with concern, looking from one to the other.

"Your father just demolished my No Smoking Pledge," Killian said, pushing to her feet. "Starting tomorrow, I should be back to a pack a day."

"Glad to ruin you, kiddo."

She was actually touched by the endearment. With a wave she started back toward Hannah's cottage. A couple of seconds later, she was surprised to find Perth walking her to the kitchen door.

"What happened?"

"Fell off the wheelchair coming out to smoke his cigar. I saw him from my window."

"Thanks," he said softly as they reached the door.

"No problem."

He didn't walk away. They were immersed in the shadow of the house. Killian looked at the dark grass and the road and sky. She looked at everything except Perth, only a step away.

"Are you okay?"

"About?" She looked up into his handsome face. His hair was wet. The shirt was spotted by water.

"About the cemetery. Your mother's grave." He placed his hand on her shoulder. She could feel the warmth of his touch through the sweatshirt. She didn't back away. "You were pretty upset. I'm sorry I took you there with no warning."

He smelled like the sea, like the ocean breeze after a storm. Her heart was racing out of control. If they stood there another second, she knew he would kiss her. Or she would kiss him.

"I...I'll live," she murmured, escaping into the house.

CHAPTER 13

"Your father is not only charming, but funny, too," Killian told Perth after he finished with the touchups and inspection of the rest of the cottage and joined her in the living room. The front wall was all they had left to paint.

"Don't spread it around," Perth said under his breath.

"Let me guess. He's got a reputation to protect, too?"

"Something like that."

"So the pineapple doesn't fall far from the tree."

"Pineapples don't grow on trees."

"No. Really?"

Today, the corners of Perth's green eyes were easy to crease into the hint of a smile. He picked up the painter's cap Killian had tossed to the floor and pulled it backward over her head.

"You wear more of this stuff than you get on the walls."

He was doing it to her again. Standing close. Touching her casually. Totally messing with her head. Killian held her breath momentarily as he used a clean rag to dab at a glob of paint she had on her chin. She didn't care if there was really any paint there or not. The sleeveless green tee-shirt stretched over the muscular chest almost matched the color of his eyes. Her cheeks burned as he studied every inch of her face.

"You two seem to have a good relationship," Killian said, searching desperately for something to say.

"Yeah, we do. Actually, it's better than good." He picked up his roller and started painting where she'd already cut in along the ceiling and a window.

Walt was paraplegic. That had to create complications. Killian was impressed with the way Perth spoke about and treated his father. And with the way his father talked about him. She'd seen some of that last night.

"What I said the other day about not being able to leave the island because of Walt. That was wrong," Perth told her. "He's never held me back. He wants me to go. But I can't do it. He's my only family."

"How old were you at the time of the accident?"

"Almost two."

"So you have no memory of your mother?"

He shook his head. "And for as long as I can remember, Walt's been in a wheelchair."

"That had to be tough, raising a toddler. Did he have help?"

"Some, I guess. Neighbors. Friends. We had family, but that was cut off when we moved to the island. He just always took the lion's share, anyway. He was a single parent and did it all. And he took good care of me, regardless of not having the use of his legs."

Killian used a brush to cut in the paint around the doorframe, trying to keep one step ahead of him.

"He pretty much raised a child on his own, but you don't think he can handle you moving to the mainland for college? It's not like you're going away forever."

Perth shrugged. "I don't know. I don't feel right about it. But maybe when the time comes—when I know I *have* to go—it'll be easier. I guess it's just the bird testing his wings and leaving the nest."

"In your case, there are no wings. Just fins," Killian said, sending him a side glance. "You'll be winning a dozen gold medals in the Olympics, and I'll be plastering your posters all over my walls. I'll spend all my time trying to convince people that I was the girl who fell off a cliff the height of Eiffel Tower and was saved by the amazing Perth Jonson."

"That reminds me." He laid the roller down in the pan and met her gaze. "Give me a couple of hours, and I'll teach you how to swim."

"It's going to take more than couple of hours with me. I'm terrified of the water. And after that fall, I now have emotional scars."

"Give me some credit. I'm a professional. We'll start with a couple of hours and see where that takes us."

Killian wasn't stupid enough to think he was asking her on a date. Still, the idea of just the two of them on the beach sounded like something she wouldn't mind trying out.

Voices. Two girls outside the cottage.

"Which one?"

"Right there?"

"You're sure."

"Jeez. I saw him this morning."

"Don't come in and spoil it for me."

"I won't. But you have to ask him out. Right away."

They both turned toward the door at the sound of someone coming up the porch steps. Killian put the brush down on the pan and pulled off her gloves, but Perth went back to rolling the paint.

A young woman breezed in, carrying an oversized basket packed with housekeeping stuff. Towels, toilet articles, supplies for the cottage.

"Wow, this is a fun job." The newcomer shifted the basket onto one hip and stared at Perth's back. She glanced once at Killian and then back to Perth.

Tall, too thin, but still athletic-looking. Blond hair pulled into a ponytail. Only a touch of makeup on a perfect doll-shaped face. She looked to be around Killian's age.

"Can I help you out with that?" Killian asked, moving closer.

"Yeah. That'll be great." The young woman handed the basket over. "I'm Brittany. Brittany Kemper. Just started an hour ago."

"Killian."

"I figured. Elena told me all about you." She stepped past her. "Hi, Perth."

"Brittany." He never stopped or looked over his shoulder.

"All of a sudden, you're a celebrity. I think it is so dope that you've been in all the papers. I cut out the large picture of you and your father that was in the *Boston Globe*. Will you autograph it for me?"

"Yeah, right."

Turning her back on them, Killian carried the basket to the kitchenette area and started to take the supplies out. Apparently, Brittany didn't hear any sarcasm in Perth's tone.

"The most recent article said that you skipped the state invitational meet, but you were still invited to compete at the Olympic swimming trials in Nebraska at the end of this month," she said excitedly. "You're going, aren't you?"

Taking his time to put the roller back in the tray, Perth didn't answer right away. But it didn't matter, because Brittany just kept on rolling.

"The article said you have a lock on the 1500 meter freestyle and the 10K marathon swim. And that's not only for the US team. They're talking about gold in the Olympics, too!"

Killian put the empty basket on the floor by the door and went back to the kitchen area. She'd only been kidding about the Olympics. She felt a little bit foolish not knowing he really was that good. Whatever Perth's reservations were about leaving the island, it sounded like his aquatic talents were clearly going to take care of it.

"Why this interest in swimming all of a sudden?" Perth straightened up and wiped his hands on a rag. "You could take or leave it last summer."

"What do you mean? I'm going to be the captain of the girls swim team at my school in Falmouth, this year. Isn't that way cool?"

"Great."

"Hey, I've got to get back to the inn before Elena has a coronary, but do you want to go swimming after work?"

"I can't."

"How about tomorrow? I'd love to have you help me with my strokes."

Killian glanced at Perth over Brittany's nicely tanned shoulder. He was standing with his back to the wall and clearly at a loss for how to respond.

"Uh…maybe," he managed to say.

"Awesome!" Brittany nearly squealed. "Well, see you later."

Snatching up the basket, she practically sailed out of the cottage.

Killian picked up her gloves and paintbrush.

"Killian?"

"Yes?" She dipped her brush into the can and accidentally dabbed the door frame with paint. She carefully wiped it off with her glove.

"'Maybe' means 'maybe'. Isn't that right?"

"That's what I hear," she said, focusing on the wall.

CHAPTER 14

The call to her father's cell phone went straight to his voicemail. Killian didn't leave a message.

Sunday morning, 8:00 a.m. She guessed he had already been up for an hour with the twins. Susan always insisted that they all go to church at ten, but she wouldn't get out of bed until nine. So there was no chance she'd be answering the phone. She dialed the home number. Her father answered on the second ring.

"Dad. It's Killian."

"What's wrong?"

"Nothing," she lied, remembering the pact she'd made with herself overnight. She wouldn't bring up her mother's grave. Not in the first minute of the conversation, anyway.

"Oh, good. Do you need money?"

"No. There's nothing to spend money on out here. Besides, I should have my first paycheck this coming week."

The sound of screeching boys echoed into the receiver. She could imagine the toddlers wrestling on his lap.

"I was wondering if I was going to hear from you. Don't you check your email anymore?"

"Actually, I haven't figured out how to get Internet out here. Why?"

"No problem. I'll overnight you the forms."

"What forms?" she asked. The screams on the other end were growing louder. She had to repeat the question.

"For your PG year. I decided on what you'll be doing next year."

"Another year of high school?" she asked incredulously.

"Come in, Killian. You're only seventeen. A post-graduate year will do you a lot of good. And it'll give you a place to be while you figure what you want to do."

"Dad, I've already graduated. There's no way I'm going to repeat my last year of high school."

She could hear the muffled orders of her father trying to separate the little monsters. The phone dropped with a bang. A second later he picked it up.

"Look, I can't talk now. But I'm sending the application overnight. Slap an essay on it, sign the thing, and send it right back. I already talked to Admissions at Green Mountain, so this is all just formality. You're in." He started talking to the twins about their choice of pancakes or French toast. He came back on the line. "Hey, call me next week."

"No, Dad," she said heatedly. "Going back to Vermont is not an option. You don't have to worry about what I'll be doing next year."

Killian realized she was talking to a dead line. He'd already hung up. Anger simmered in her veins. Another year of high school? He was out of his mind. Tears threatened to spill over. She heard Elena coming into the kitchen. Using the phone was perfectly fine with the innkeeper, but now Killian wished she'd never made the call. She blinked back her tears and slipped into the laundry room, checking for any clothes in the dryer. There were towels that needed to be folded.

"Were you able to reach your father?" Elena asked, looking in from the kitchen. She was carrying a basket of cut flowers.

"Yeah. Thank you."

"Everything okay?" she asked.

"Great."

"You can always leave this number with him. Just in case he wants to get hold of you."

She wouldn't. He wouldn't.

"Thanks," Killian said politely.

Elena watched her in silence for a couple of moments. It was impossible for Killian to hide how miserable she felt.

"Oh. Some of the people from the State checked in last night. They wanted breakfast sent down to the first cottage. I know you came in early today, but...would you mind?"

"No. I'll take the tray down to them," Killian replied, happy for the chance to get out from under the magnifying glass. She needed to get busy if she was going to shake off this rotten mood.

Elena was a whirlwind in the kitchen. By the time Killian finished folding the towels and putting them away upstairs, the innkeeper had a double tray stacked and ready to go.

"The older man's name is Davenport. I believe he's the head researcher. There's a graduate student already checked into the same cottage. If you want, you can look up his name in the register."

It didn't matter. Killian grabbed the trays and headed out. Going down the path, she took her time, forcing air into her lungs and trying to steady her breathing. A PG year. He was just making sure she wouldn't be hanging around the house, come September 1st. Or Susan was.

She was totally screwed. Well, she wasn't going back to Vermont. Clearly, she couldn't go back to Connecticut, either. But how many jobs were there for a seventeen year old high school graduate with no experience? Jobs that paid enough to cover rent and food? Not too many. She didn't know how she could possibly survive.

Not doing anything last year about going to college suddenly topped the list of stupid decisions she'd made in life. Another year in Vermont. She was mad as hell at her father. And his lie about Ama's body wasn't even in her top five reasons any more.

By the time Killian reached the cottage, she'd stretched a tarp over her raw emotions and tucked it in tightly. A middle-aged man was standing outside on the porch. Plastic storage bins were stacked along the wall by the door. A computer cord was draped over his shoulder, and he was shuffling the containers around, looking behind them.

"Mr. Davenport?" she said, trying to not startle him.

"Doctor," he replied, straightening up and looking at her.

"Oh, sorry. Good morning, Dr. Davenport."

UMass baseball hat, untrimmed salt-and-pepper beard, wire-rimmed glasses. He looked the part of the scientist. He waved the cord at her.

"Sorry, there are no plugs outside. I guess you can run an extension cord out through the window."

He dropped the cord on a chair and moved a bunch of spiral-bound notebooks off the table. "That must be our breakfast."

Killian was careful not to tip the tray on the last step of the delivery. As she set up the dishes and napkins and silverware on the table, he called inside the door to someone that the food had arrived. He turned to her and took out his wallet.

"That's okay. Elena handles the room charge."

"It's a tip." He held out a five dollar bill to her.

"Thanks." Killian took it, wondering whether they had a system for sharing tips. She made a mental note to ask Elena.

"So, did they finish painting these cottages five minutes before we got here?"

"Pretty much," she said, turning to go. "I'll be back for the dishes later."

"What's your name?"

She stopped by the porch stairs. "Killian."

"How old are you, Killian?"

"Seventeen."

"High school?"

"Just graduated."

"Early. You must be smart. From where?"

"Green Mountain Academy in Vermont."

"Congratulations." He focused on her more closely. "So where are you headed for college?"

Killian hated that question. Ever since April and when her classmates all got their college acceptance letters, she'd been asked this same question over and over again. And she'd been stumbling for an answer to it. She didn't know why adults—even strangers—thought they had the right to know.

"I'm taking a gap year," she finally answered.

Thankfully, he seemed to lose interest in her college plans. He took the cover off the plate of toast and eggs.

"I'll come by later and pick up the dishes." She started backing up.

"Are you local, Killian?" he asked.

"Only here for the summer."

"Do you know any of the islanders?"

"I just arrived this past week, but I've met a handful of people."

"Where do you live?"

One too many questions, she thought. He was just about to cross into the creep category.

"Up the road," she answered vaguely, stepping down from the porch.

"Know someone named Walter Jonson?"

She hesitated. There was probably no harm in answering his question. There were so few people living year round on the island that it'd be very easy to find anyone. But something about the guy was starting to irk her.

"Are you a friend of his?" she asked.

"An old acquaintance." He laid his knife and fork down on the tray. "Do you know him?"

"I think I've heard the name."

"Know where he lives?"

"No." Killian shook her head, backing up on the grass.

He stood up and reached into his wallet again. This time he took out a ten dollar bill, holding it out to her. "I'm going to be busy here this morning, so I can't hunt him down myself. Find out where he lives and there'll be ten more."

She waved him off and started to walk away. "That's okay. I can find out without a tip."

"When will you get back to me?" he called as she started walking away.

"When the hell freezes over," she whispered under her breath.

CHAPTER 15

"Seriously. You know we're going to have a *ton* of work once the summer really starts," Brittany pleaded, carrying a tray of salt and pepper shakers into the dining room. "Can't I *please* have the afternoon off?"

"No," Elena said firmly. "You only started yesterday, and I have *tons* for all of you to do *now*."

Killian moved the pile of cloth napkins she'd been folding onto one of the tables so that Brittany had a place to put down the tray. This was the first time all four of the summer help were working in the same room. The innkeeper had them cleaning and setting up the smaller dining room overlooking the harbor. She wanted to start serving meals here tonight.

"Come on, Elena," Brittany whined in a practiced tone. "I have a *really* special date this afternoon."

Killian glanced at Amanda, the quietest one of the three, and the young woman rolled her eyes. It was a relief to know there was someone hovering on the edge of 'normal' among her workmates. Amanda seemed like someone Killian could actually be friends with.

Brittany's sidekick Liz was mouthing encouragement to her friend behind Elena's back.

"*Please?* It's really special."

Elena shook her head. "A *really* special guy will wait until five o'clock for you to get out of work."

"But we were going swimming."

"Sorry. I need you here."

Killian did not want to let her feelings show regarding Brittany's plans. Keeping her back to the persistent young woman, she moved from table to table, arranging the napkins. She didn't want to dwell on the fact that Perth was the special guy Brittany planned to spend the afternoon with. She knew he'd given her less than minimum encouragement. Still, it annoyed her to think Brittany would be pursuing him at every turn.

"Elena?"

"End of discussion," the innkeeper said sharply, obviously very comfortable managing teenagers. "Plates and silverware. And I want one of those hurricane lamps on every table."

A few more of the people working on the wind farm project were checking in today. Killian's understanding was that even those bunking on the research vessel docked in the harbor planned to have most of their meals at the inn.

"Where are you supposed to meet him?" Liz whispered to Brittany when Elena disappeared toward a supply closet.

"And what time?" Amanda added.

"I don't know. We didn't set a time or place," Brittany answered. "But I know he's not working here today. When I get out, I'll find him."

"You can always stop at his house after work and leave a message to meet you at the lighthouse tonight," Liz suggested. "Everyone will be there."

"That doesn't work. I did that a few times last year, and he never showed up."

"Last year, you had no boobs. Now you've got the killer bod." Liz reached across the table and grabbed for her breasts.

Brittany laughed and slapped her friend's hands away. "I'm not looking for a party at the lighthouse. I want some one-on-one."

"Oh, you'll get your one-on-one, alright." Amanda raised her eyebrows suggestively up and down.

The proverbial wallflower. This was the way it always was with Killian whenever she was around kids her own age. Barely seen and hardly included. In this case, she was extremely happy about it.

Elena came in with a stack of dishes. "Killian, would you give me a hand and take these to the kitchen?"

"Sure." She grabbed a tray, piled the dishes on it, and followed Elena out.

It wasn't until they were in the kitchen that Killian realized she'd been clenching her jaw so tight that the muscles in her face hurt. The phone conversation with her father. The annoying *Dr.* Davenport. Listening to these moronic girls in the dining room. So far, this was turning out to be a one-star day, at best.

"I want you to run an errand for me this afternoon."

Killian put the dishes down on the counter and turned around. "Glad to do it." She'd go anywhere, so long as she didn't have to hear any more about Brittany and Perth's budding fantasy romance.

"Do you know how to get to the salt pond?"

Perth was the first thing that came to her mind. She hadn't seen him since yesterday. He'd mentioned there was a lot to do at the salt pond and that's where he was going today.

"I take the road past the town dump?"

"That's right. I want you to take my golf cart. Perth should be there. I need two bushels of oysters for dinner tonight."

Killian thought for a second about the wild-looking old man out there. She'd mentioned Lynx to her aunt last night. Hannah, too, assured her that he was harmless.

"No problem," she finally said. "Anything else you want me to pick up while I'm out?"

Elena looked over her shoulder, making sure none of the other girls were within earshot. "You've been doing your part. I want you to stay at the salt pond and enjoy the afternoon. There's a really nice sandy beach out there."

Killian knew exactly where that beach was.

"And I don't need you back with the shellfish until five. Go."

She didn't need to be asked twice.

Four hours off.

Killian knew she was living in LaLa Land, thinking that Perth would want to sit around on a beach with her. Still, she swung by the house and slipped a bathing suit on under her regular clothes. Her aunt wasn't home. She grabbed a bag of snacks.

Before leaving, she knocked on Walt's door, but there was no answer. She wanted to tell him about the guest at the inn who was asking questions about him. Davenport was probably just an old friend of Walt's, but she didn't particularly like his manner. And after the conversation with her father, she'd been in no mood to be friendly.

To play it safe, Killian wrote a two-line note to Walter and slipped it through the mail slot.

The road to the town dump wound around and over hills and through groves of trees. After leaving the cluster of houses by the harbor, the path was just two parallel dirt tracks and no wider in places than the width of the town truck. Bumping along in the inn's golf cart, Killian enjoyed the feel of the salt breeze in her hair. It was nice of Elena to push her out the door this way. Especially after saying 'no' to Brittany.

The sky was pale blue and the sun brilliant. Earlier, she'd noticed there were at least a dozen more sailboats and motorboats in the harbor than yesterday. Hannah had mentioned that the population of the island went from the fifty year-round folks to around four or five hundred in the summertime, with some weekends higher than that. Summer cottages belonging to islanders were rented out, and a handful of larger houses owned by mainlanders were leased for the season to groups of people. Killian already overheard that the girls working with her at the inn were renting one of those houses with some of the other summer help.

At a bend in the road, Killian caught a glimpse of the Tower through a break in the trees. As she was looking at the gray stone structure, the cart dove into a huge dip in the road. The two white buckets Elena had given her for the shellfish went clattering out the back. Killian slammed on the brake, set it, and jumped out to get them.

Not even twenty yards back, the containers sat on their sides. Walking toward them, she peered into the dense woods. Branches of trees overhead wove shadows on the road. The motor of the cart made no noise, and the silence was only broken by the sound of waves in the distance and the soft breeze rustling through the leaves. She hadn't seen anyone since leaving the village. But that was no different from the first day she'd come wandering out at this end of the island.

There would be no missing the salt pond. She knew this road ended at it. But Killian had been paying little attention to time or distance. She had no clue how near or far she was from the water.

She picked up the containers and stacked them inside each other. Turning around, she stopped dead.

Old Lynx stood by her cart, facing her.

He looked the same as the first time she'd seen him. Same ragged clothes, same walking stick. Learning as much as she had about the man didn't lessen her nervousness at all. He was still terrifying. It was a struggle not to drop everything and start running.

"I'm on my way to get some shellfish for the inn," Killian said aloud, hoping to keep any note of fear out of her voice.

With unseeing eyes, he simply stared.

He is *not* dangerous, she told herself. The first time they'd met, he hadn't pushed her off the cliff. She'd slipped on the rocks. Maybe she could just walk past him to the cart.

Or maybe not.

"Elena wants me back right away."

"You saw the room in the Tower."

Everyone said Lynx couldn't speak. But he could. He's spoken to her before. He was speaking to her now.

"You saw the Mark of Five."

"Yeah, I saw it." Killian didn't want to believe there was any significance in the pentagram. Not the way Perth tried to connect it to her.

"You were born to it."

"How could I be born to a shape? I'm no different than a dozen teenagers who are working for the summer on this island." Killian couldn't believe that she was actually arguing with the ragged stranger.

"They're using you."

"Who's using me?"

A car was coming up the path. She glanced fleetingly over her shoulder. The grinding sound of the engine told her it was the same pickup truck that made a regular run for the dump.

Killian turned around. The cart was sitting where she'd left it.

Lynx was gone.

CHAPTER 16

"Lynx doesn't talk."

"He might not talk to you or Hannah or other people, but he's a chatterbox with me."

Killian dropped the two buckets by the edge of the salt pond. Perth had tried to carry them from the cart, but she didn't let him.

"What did he say?"

She forced herself to stare out at the lines of posts just off the beach, rather than at him. He was wearing only shorts, and it was very difficult to concentrate on being angry at anything or anyone when he was standing right there, looking *that* good.

"He said I was born to it. You know, the thing in the Tower. The birthmark on my back."

"The pentagram."

"If he can't see, how does he know what the floor looks like up there?" She shot a look at the Tower, high on the cliff. "And how would he know about my birthmark, anyway? Do you think he was watching us the day you dragged me out of the water?"

"Hey, even *you* agree that he's blind. So I don't know how he'd know."

"Well, this is a strange island. You can 'fix' people. And all the way out here, I can hear a fly buzzing back in my bedroom. I'm thinking Lynx chooses who he wants to talk to and maybe what he wants to see."

Perth's expression became serious. Killian guessed his mood would change any second now, and he'd bark at her. Or ask her to leave. She hadn't even mentioned Lynx's comment about people using her. She had no clue what he meant by it.

"Never mind what I just said."

He was still brooding.

She twisted around and looked at her butt. "I wonder if I can surgically remove this thing, so you and Lynx can be both happy."

He tapped her on the shoulder. "*You* are not the problem."

She was relieved to see the smile back in his face.

"Oysters." She motioned toward the bins at her feet. "Get to work."

"When do you have to be back at the inn?"

"By five." Killian reached into her pocket and took out a wristwatch she'd stuffed there earlier. She hated wearing the thing, but without her cell phone, she'd resorted to carrying around the old reliable to keep track of time. "It's two-thirty already."

"Okay, let's go."

"Let's go where?"

"Get your oysters." He nodded toward the salt pond. "They're right here. You can help."

"Seriously?" She looked out at the lines of posts. "Those are too far from the beach. I can't go out there. I'll drown."

He shook his head in disbelief. "With the tide out, the water is only knee deep."

She gauged the distance again. It couldn't be that shallow. "Knee deep for you is neck high for me. And what happens if the tide comes in fast? And how flat is the bottom of that pond? Are there any valleys? Or riptides? Or sharks?"

She screeched when he picked her up by the waist and started for the water.

"No! Don't! My work clothes."

"Too late."

"I have a bathing suit underneath."

He put her back on her feet. "Okay, take your clothes off."

A couple more minutes of this kind of talk and he'd have to spoon her off the sand.

It was pointless to tell him to turn around or to admit she was shy about taking off her clothes while he watched her. She was on a beach, and she was wearing a bathing suit under her tee-shirt and shorts. Once again, she was making too much out of nothing.

"Clothes or not, on the count of five, I'm dragging you in the water with me."

Killian kicked her shoes off. She turned her back to him and quickly peeled off her shirt and shorts.

"You're being bossy. I think it's your job to get the shellfish, not mine."

She turned around and whatever she was saying went right out of her head. He wasn't just watching her. He was taking total inventory of her body.

All of a sudden, every penny she'd spent on the white bikini she bought a year ago…and never wore…was worth it.

Killian walked past him to the pond's edge. "I better not get wet past my knees, or there'll be hell to pay."

Perth walked in behind her. He took her hand. "That's a lot of tough talk."

"I know. And I mean it, too."

The water temperature was absolutely perfect, and she could see right to the bottom. Killian tried to not let her eyes linger on the tan, muscular arms next to her pale skin as they walked side by side. She tried not to gloat that she was here and spending a couple of hours with Perth on the beach. But she did let herself wonder for just a moment what Brittany—with all her wheedling charm and boy-savvy—was doing back at the inn.

The oyster beds were to their left. Half a dozen steps into the water and Killian realized he was leading her away from them and straight into the deeper water.

"Perth?" She tried to pull free.

"Killian?" he replied, mimicking her tone and pulling her until she was forced to take a large step forward.

The bottom suddenly fell away. There was nothing for her to step on. She sank into the pond, but before her head could go under, he caught her by the waist.

"How could you?" Her arms flew around his neck, practically choking him. Her feet kicked at the colder water below the surface, searching for solid ground. His legs were the only thing she felt.

"I'm going to kill you," she sputtered. "Hear me? Murder you. You tricked me."

"Killian, relax."

His face was an inch away. He was smiling.

"You relax, fish boy. This is no way to—"

He kissed her. A soft kiss on the lips that teased her with the promise of more. A lot more.

Killian restrained herself from attacking him right there. Their bodies were tangled together in the water. There was a sharp-edged glint of desire in his green eyes that she'd seen on the beach, too. This was all too new to her, actually wanting someone to touch her, kiss her. Even at the handful of parties she'd gone to during high school, she'd used every excuse she could think of to keep the boys from getting too touchy feely. This was different.

"Is this part of your 'give me two hours and I'll teach you how to swim' plan?"

"Sort of."

Her gaze moved from his straight nose and chiseled jaw to the drops of water glistening on his full lips. She looked into his eyes. Whatever way she looked at him, Perth was perfection, and Killian hoped he'd kiss her again.

Her grip around his neck loosened. He had no trouble keeping them both afloat.

"What do you mean 'sort of'?"

"I'm redirecting your subconscious."

"My subconscious?" she asked, trying to reconnect all the brain cells she'd lost the moment his lips touched hers.

"To keep you from panicking when you get in the water."

"That sink-or-swim approach does not work for me. Group lessons, private instruction, camp, whatever. I was taught the mechanics so many times. My parents tried everything. I'm just afraid of drowning. And no one can help me."

"But that only makes sense," he responded, smiling. "Drowning would be a bad thing."

"Exactly."

"But I can help you." He pulled her closer, stealing another kiss.

"You're not taking me seriously, are you?" Killian said, forcing back a groan of delight and frustration.

"I really am," he said smiling. "You see, I've already rewired your brain."

Killian forgot whatever it was she'd been planning to say as Perth floated an arm length's away. A second of panic and her head dipped under, but then he was right there. Holding her above the surface.

"Take a deep breath and hold it."

He eased her down into the water again and went with her. She sank beneath the surface, but she could see his reassuring face in front of hers. Still underwater, he kissed her again and then backed away, pointing upward. Killian kicked her feet a couple of times and began to move, following him toward the sunlight.

She was *not* a hundred twenty pound rock about to sink to the bottom of the salt pond. She felt like she was floating on the clouds.

"You have it," he said, taking hold of Killian's waist and bringing her flush against his body. "Next time, we'll start some actual swim lessons."

She was disappointed when her feet brushed against the sandy bottom. He let her go, but her knees were unsteady. It took her a moment before she could come close to taking a step.

"Ready to help me get those oysters for Elena?"

Oysters? Who cares about oysters? The air around her was just a delicious blur. Her lips tingled. Her heartbeat was still few notches above marathon pace. Killian took his outstretched hand and tried to clear the drugging effect his kisses had on her. There was no hope.

"So explain this to me. What just happened?"

"A lot of people can't swim because of some bad memory. Something scary happened, having to do with the water. Maybe something terrible."

"If there ever was such a thing, I don't remember it. I just know that when I step in, I panic."

"Exactly. Water is a stimulus." They waded toward the shellfish beds. "Like I said, I redirected your subconscious. I tried to connect being in the water with a pleasant experience."

Killian felt the heat still in her lips.

"So the next time, you won't be driven by some repressed fear. You'll think of me."

"You are pretty sure of yourself, aren't you?"

"Did it work?"

She couldn't argue with that. "But how do you know my fear isn't stronger than your kisses?"

He stopped and faced her, his gaze drifting down to her lips. "We can try it again, to make sure."

Killian wanted to so badly. But she didn't trust herself. She didn't think she could make him stop if he kissed her again. She didn't think she could make herself stop. The tingling she was feeling was not just in her lips. Her entire body was electric.

"Jeez, you're like some homeopathic doctor. You fix the head, the body, the whole shebang. You got a license to practice medicine, Doc?"

He laughed, bringing her hand to his lips before letting go. "You wait here. Keep an eye open for riptides and sharks."

They were standing by the oyster beds in knee-deep water. Killian watched him as he moved off. She could see her feet on the sandy bottom. Little schools of fish were swimming around her.

These past few days totally defied logic. She'd gone from sulking and unhappy on the mainland to this. She was actually happy.

Watching him, she realized there were cables running between the posts under the water. Black bins the size of laundry baskets hung from them. Each bin had a top and holes that water could flow through.

He looked over at her. "Come and see this."

Killian waded toward him. "I grew up in Connecticut. Went to high school in the hills of Vermont. Can you tell me what you're doing here?"

"Aquaculture."

"You told me that already."

"Growing shellfish under controlled conditions."

"Like gardening," she said.

"Exactly."

He led her to a larger, submerged box at one end of a line of poles. He pulled a screen off the top and she looked inside. At first, she thought she was just looking at sand at the bottom. Then she realized there had to be millions of what looked like shiny, irregular-shaped, little specks.

"Are these baby oysters?"

Perth took few out and put them in the palm of her hand.

"We call them seeds. I got them just two weeks ago."

"You buy them?"

"Yeah. You place an order with a hatchery."

"Like where they raise chicks?" she teased.

"Just about. They have adult shellfish spawn in temperature-controlled tanks, producing thousands of larvae. Then they give the larvae a diet of algae until they're big enough to ship. I grow them in here and then move them to the bins that are hanging on those lines between the posts."

Killian looked at the length and width of the area Perth was using. This close, it seemed huge. "You must buy a lot of seeds."

"No. Not really," he told her. "An empty soda-can holds a hundred thousand animals. After one year, a six-pack of seed cans could fill half of a ten-wheeler truck. That's over half a million oysters, if the conditions allow it."

Killian thought about how expensive oysters were in the restaurants.

"Do you own all of this?"

"This is a co-op. Owned by a handful of people on the island. My father and I are only partners."

"But you do all the physical labor part of it?"

He shrugged. "It's not a problem. We have an arrangement."

"Can anyone start a business like this?"

"It's easier said than done. You need a place to set it up and a permit. And you need federal and state approval to be granted a license to work the tidal flats. Farms are only licensed where the water is clean."

She looked around them. There were no boats in the salt pond. No tourists. On the far side of the island from the harbor and no good roads in between, there was nothing to draw people here.

He moved down the beds. She followed him. He lifted a line and took a good-sized oyster out of a bin and handed it to her. The shell was about three inches across.

"That's more like what I've seen in stores and restaurants."

"This is the final harvest."

"How long from the seeds to this?"

"About three years."

She looked up, surprised. "That's a long time."

"Exactly," he said quietly. "Long hours, six days a week, working eight or nine months a year in all kinds of weather. I enjoy the job, but I'm not ready to spend the rest of my life doing it."

His green eyes focused on her face.

"I understand why you might want to leave."

Perth dipped his head and their lips touched. This time, the kiss lingered, the heat building. She became more of an instigator than a follower, slipping her arms around his waist and pulling herself against him. They were both breathless when he pulled away.

"Well," he said a moment later. "You seem to be the only one who understands."

Killian wanted to spend the rest of the day with Perth. But she couldn't. She had to get back to the inn. He had more work left to do at the pond. And then there was his nightly long distance swim.

Lying in bed that night, she welcomed the distant hum of noises. The clap and ring of rigging against sailboat masts. The far off laughter of people. The bark of a dog. This was the happiest she'd been in years. For the first time ever, she felt like she belonged.

She thought about how crazy a day it had been. Dinner at the inn had been fast, and she'd managed to stay in the kitchen helping Elena while Dr. Davenport and the other researchers were eating.

Her coworker Amanda—the quiet one—had invited Killian to go along with her to the lighthouse to where the young crowd would be gathering to party tonight. Killian made up some lame excuse and went home to have supper with Hannah. She just didn't want to be part of that scene.

Right now, at this moment, replaying in her mind the hours she'd spent with Perth on the beach, she was enjoying one of the greatest feelings she'd had for a long time.

Killian heard the bang of a screen door and the sound of Walt's wheelchair rolling down the ramp. His nightly cigar. She was tempted to put some clothes on and go join him outside. She enjoyed his wit and gruff attitude. She appreciated his honesty. Sitting in bed, she wondered if he'd mind the company.

Before she could get up, Killian heard footsteps coming up the lane. She didn't have to look out the window to know they didn't belong to Perth or Hannah. Perth's steps were soft and fluid. He was like a cat on the prowl. When he was barefoot, he walked more on the grass than in the lane. Hannah's steps were short and quick. Her heels scuffed the ground as she walked.

These steps were confident and heavy; this was a man on a mission. The footsteps went by Hannah's cottage and stopped next door.

"Walter? Walter Jonson?"

Killian immediately recognized the voice. Davenport. She hadn't told the researcher where Walt lived. But somebody had.

Perth's father said nothing.

"Dr. Davenport. I know you remember me."

"Should I?"

Killian recalled the note she'd left next door in the mail drop. She'd mentioned the man's name.

"Come on, Walter." There was a twinge of impatience in the tone. "I was your doctor. How long ago was it? Almost twenty years. But I know you remember me."

Curious, Killian got out of bed and looked out the window. From where she was, she could only see shadowy figures of the men.

There was a long silence.

"Mass General. Clinical trial studies," Davenport snapped. "Early genetic mutation."

"What can I do for you?" Walt asked in a cool voice.

"To start, you can tell me what the hell happened to you?"

"The wheelchair? An accident."

"I know about the accident. I saw you right before you were released from the hospital. And then...poof! You disappeared off the face of the earth."

"I moved."

"And you didn't bother to tell me you were moving," Davenport said shortly. "You left us no forwarding address."

"Oh, *that's* why I stopped getting Christmas cards."

"We needed to know where you were. You should have let us know."

"I don't recall signing anything about that."

"You were part of a study."

"Funny, I seem to remember seeing articles later on referring to your little study. Not very positive."

"Reporters blow things out of proportion. Everyone knew there were risks involved."

"Don't get me wrong," Walt said. "You were always clear that there were no guarantees. But I believe even your colleagues used terms like 'quackery' and 'rogue medicine.'"

"I don't care what the hell they said. We were on the cutting edge of science." Davenport was struggling to regain his cool when he continued. "You could have done me the courtesy of notifying us that you were ending your participation."

"Well, what can I say? Sorry. I didn't. Here we are. Twenty years later. Don't you have anything better to do than go around slapping your ex-patients' hands?"

"Ex-patients? There are no ex-patients. Everyone died. I thought you had, too."

"Sorry to disappoint you."

"You did, by disappearing," Davenport snapped, his temper flaring again. "They said my work was a failure. I lost my research funding. My license was revoked. My reputation destroyed. They ended the study. All of it came to a dead stop. I needed one case, one patient, who responded to the treatment. And you were here all the time."

The silence in the night was alive, charged.

Another scratch of the lighter. Walter lighting another cigar.

"I couldn't help you, Doc."

"What do you mean, you couldn't help me?" The pitch of his voice rose. "Here you are alive. Years beyond any reasonable expectation. But you couldn't help me?"

"Now, isn't it just a little bit arrogant of you to assume that it was *your* treatment that has kept me alive?"

"Okay, then tell me. What other doctor have you been seeing? What treatments have you had? You owe me at least that."

"I owe you nothing," Walt's tone matched Davenport's. "What I did or didn't do and why I'm not six feet under is none of your business. We're done talking here."

The sound of the wheelchair on the ramp. Walt was going back to the house.

"You have a son," Davenport called after him. "I saw a picture of him with you in the *Boston Globe* not too long ago."

"Is that how you found me?"

"That's how I knew you were alive. And yes, where you live," Davenport admitted. "I needed to get the university to pull just a few strings to land this wind project job with the State. After what happened, I didn't want anyone saying that I came out here to harass you."

"You've gone to heck of a lot of trouble for nothing."

"I don't consider resurrecting my name and reputation nothing."

"Goodbye, Dr. Davenport." The chair started rolling up the ramp again.

"Perth is an athlete. You know he's looking at the same death sentence if he has the mutation."

The wheelchair paused.

"You and your wife knew the rules. The mutation passes on to offspring ninety percent of the time. Short life expectancy. No children."

Walt started up the ramp again.

"Has he been tested?"

The rolling wheels on the ramp were the only response.

"Does he know?"

The screen door slammed.

CHAPTER 17

"Of all the beautiful places that I could take you around this island, I can't believe this is where you wanted to come. But maybe I can."

Killian and Hannah stood by the entrance of the cemetery. She had to practically drag her aunt here this afternoon. Killian had a couple of hours off before dinner at the inn.

The heartbreak of what she'd heard last night between Walt and Davenport was weighing heavily on her mind. The thought that Perth could be sick--that he could die young--clawed open a very painful wound. She had stopped to see her mother's grave on the way to work this morning. That's when Killian had noticed a few other things.

The mystery of this place was bad enough. The significance of the inner, walled graveyard only added another troubling puzzle. The loose ends were countless. The handful of happy moments she'd spent with Perth yesterday had been replaced with fear and worry. Killian needed answers.

"As you can see, there's not much here. Some old graves, family plots. It's just what you see." Hannah walked ahead of her toward the separate walled area. "There's so little to say about it."

Killian stopped her. "So many of the graves are missing dates."

"Island weather. Salt water. Wind. Erosion wears everything away."

Killian crouched before one outside of the stone wall and pulled away the thick green ivy. "This one. Henry Sutton. Look at the dates. He lived to be a hundred nineteen."

The older woman glanced at the gravestone. "That's old."

She moved to the adjacent grave. She'd spotted the date when she'd come by in the morning. "And this woman. A hundred fourteen. And I saw another one on the far side of the cemetery who lived to be a hundred twenty-four. That's not possible."

"Maybe it was a mistake."

"Could they all be mistakes?" Killian shook her head. "People don't live that long."

"Good living. Healthy lifestyle. No chemicals. No stress on the island."

None of this seemed to be a surprise to Hannah.

"I've never...*ever*...heard of anyone living that long. Have you, outside of this island?"

Hannah waved a hand and smiled. "Honey, I wouldn't fret too much about them. I'm telling you, the dates could be wrong. Folks around here weren't so much into keeping track of birth dates like mainland people are."

"But there's other weird stuff. Look at the dates that they died. They're all bunched together."

Killian went from grave to grave, pointing to the engravings. She crouched before one of them. "This husband and wife died on the same day."

"Probably epidemics. That was quite common in the past. Influenza, small pox, fevers. They could strike down half the population in an area, especially the old people." Hannah went inside the walled area of the cemetery.

Killian had hoped for a clearer answer--something that made sense. Her father's parents were in their eighties, and she considered them ancient. That was before coming here. She had no clue how old her great aunt was. But it wouldn't surprise her if Hannah was even older. And there were other questions that Killian had, too. Like why there weren't any children's graves. And the wall wasn't the only thing separating Killian's female ancestors from the other islanders. Those buried outside the walled enclosure had died old. The women inside, these women in Killian's family, all died young. Except Hannah.

She pushed to her feet and followed her great aunt. Reaching the narrow opening in stonewall, she stopped.

"Who takes care of this area?" Even the upkeep of the two sections was different. Inside the enclosure, immaculately manicured. On the other side of the wall, nature ruled.

"I told you. We all wear many hats on this island. Everyone pitches in."

"Buy why would the islanders show much more care for our family plot than the rest?" she pressed.

"More manageable?" Hannah glanced about her. "It's sort of the centerpiece of the cemetery, don't you think. Probably folks figure the hard work shows best."

There seemed to be a rehearsed answer for everything. Quick. No elaboration. Killian felt she was being lied to, but she couldn't let it show.

"Okay, here's something else. What's with the pentagrams? There're on every headstone."

"Family crest," Hannah answered, reaching for a newly sprouted weed and pulling it out of the ground. "Do you know what it signifies?"

"It's a devil cult thing, isn't it?"

"Oh no, honey. Nowadays you hear that, but it is actually a very ancient symbol, early Christian and even pre-Christian. It's the 'Endless Knot'. It signifies Truth, among other things. Our family holds that it represents the connection of everything—earth, air, fire, water, and the spirit. Your mother believed it."

Killian noticed she didn't toss the weed aside but stuffed it in her skirt pocket. "I have that mark on my back."

"So did your mother. A birthmark."

"Do you have it, too?" Killian asked.

"No, sweetheart. Tradition has it that there's only one woman in every generation blessed with the mark."

"Don't you think that's strange?"

Hannah shrugged. "It's just family legend."

Lynx knew she had the mark. Hannah knew, too. Perth's suspicion about the sign and how it was everywhere on the island was starting to make some sense.

"Who had the birthmark in your generation?"

A shadow of sadness crept into Hannah's features. Her calm appearance wavered for a moment, but she recovered quickly enough. She looked around her at the graves at their feet and moved to one not far away from Killian's mother.

"My half sister Hazel," she said softly. "Hazel Ama Winthrop."

"Your half sister?" Killian repeated.

The old woman nodded. "We shared the same father. Hazel's mother died in childbirth."

"How was Hazel related to my mother?"

"I'm your great aunt through her. You can figure it out." Hannah smiled, taking Killian by the hand and pulling her to Ama's grave. "I was thinking of planting two tea rose bushes here this fall. What color do you think your mother would have wanted?"

Killian wanted to tell Hannah she knew exactly what she was doing. She was evading any more questions.

"She loved all roses, but especially red ones."

"Red it is, then." Hannah caressed the headstone. "Maybe we won't wait for the fall, and you can help me plant them this summer."

Killian wasn't done with her questions. She wanted to know her role in all of this.

"When the time comes…when I die…will I be buried here?"

There was no pretense now. No evasion. Hannah nodded. "That's the plan."

"Will you be?"

"No, I'll be buried outside the walls with the other island folk."

Killian thought about what that all meant.

"Does that mean I'll die young like the rest of these women?"

Hannah's hand reached for hers. The fingers were strong when they squeezed hers. "You have the choice, honey. It's up to you."

CHAPTER 18

Only four tables of guests remained in the dining room. Elena assured Killian that between Amanda and Liz, they had it under control.

Brittany, Killian was certain, was home primping for a night on the prowl for Perth.

"If you could double-check the supplies in all the bathrooms on the second floor," the innkeeper continued, "and make sure all the guestrooms are ready, then you can call it a day. We have a bunch of guests arriving on the ferry tomorrow."

Killian grabbed the basket of toilet paper and soaps and shampoos from the supply closet and headed up. At the top of the stairs, she heard the voices coming from the open door of the family's apartment.

"She tripped over the rug."

"No, I didn't. It was your cat that got underfoot."

"Shadow doesn't come anywhere near you."

"I'm telling you, it was her cat."

Almost a week on the island, Killian had yet to meet Elena's mother and aunt. She knew the elderly women watched her from a distance. There were many times she'd seen a curtain move in the second story windows.

"I fell right to the floor, and my arm swelled up like a balloon."

"You tripped over the rug."

"It was the cat."

"The swelling is going down now. Your arm should be as good as new by morning."

Killian was surprised to hear Perth's voice. He was here visiting the two old ladies. She hadn't seen him since yesterday at the salt pond. Too much nonsense was rattling around in her brain. And he was the only one on this island that she could really talk to.

She missed him.

She hesitated by the door to the sisters' apartment. As much as she wanted to, she couldn't just march in.

"You're an angel, my boy."

Killian passed by, quickly moving from room to room, checking bathrooms, trying to make enough noise to have someone hear her. Nothing needed to be restocked; no one had stayed in these rooms. Everything was ready.

She paused in the hallway. Her hand rested on doorknob of the last room she had to check.

The conversation in the apartment was still dwelling on cats and rugs and how many broken bones each of the sisters had suffered from during their lifetimes. Of course, there was no consensus, at all, on any topic.

"So, what do you think of her?"

"Think of who?" Perth asked.

"Don't be coy. You know who."

"Hannah's niece. Killian," the other voice clarified.

"Well, she's beautiful."

Perth's words made her face go warm. She'd never imagined anyone referring to her that way. Not hideous, maybe. Pleasant, perhaps. Even cute. But not beautiful.

"More important, she's real. I like her a lot."

Her heart raced. Killian pushed the door open and went into the guestroom. She felt like an opportunist, listening in. At the same time, she was thrilled to know how he felt.

In the bathroom, she looked at her reflection in the mirror. Her face was flushed. Her eyes glowed. She straightened the collar of the white shirt she was wearing and pulled the elastic out of her pony tail. Soft waves of dark hair spilled around her face.

Coming back into the hall a minute later, she found the door of the apartment open. A small, plump older lady was peering out.

"Hello," Killian said politely. "I was doing a last check on the guestrooms."

The woman smiled but didn't say anything. Opening the door wide, she motioned to Killian to come in.

"Ruth, who is it?"

"Perth's girl."

Killian opened her mouth, but she didn't know what to say. The sight of Perth behind her was a relief. Sort of. She didn't think she'd ever get over how her body reacted to the sight of him.

"Bring her in. I want to meet her."

Ruth turned around and headed back inside. Killian looked up into Perth's amused expression.

"Do you have a minute to meet Lottie and Ruth?"

She put the basket of supplies down in the hall by the door. "I'm off work as of now."

As she passed by him, he leaned down and whispered in her ear.

"I knew you were out there. I totally meant what you heard me say."

Flustered, she stepped into a small living room ahead of him.

Two women sat in matching chairs covered with faded flowery material. Same hairdos, same style of dress, matching purple and pink eyeglasses with thick lenses. Ruth was plumper than her sister. Still, they could never deny they were sisters.

"Killian, this is Ruth and Lottie." Perth introduced them. "Elena's aunt and mother."

Both nodded in unison. Lottie was nursing her arm on a pillow in her lap.

"I've been meaning to stop by and introduce myself this past week," Killian said to the two women. "I'm here almost every day, so if there is—"

"How do you like Cuttylea?" Ruth interrupted.

"I like it every much."

"A second cousin, once removed, has a daughter," Lottie said. "She had childhood leukemia. She's in her twenties now and has bone cancer. Doctors have given her months to live."

Killian looked at Elena's mother. She figured these women knew how she'd lost her own mother to cancer. Friends and strangers both always did the same thing. Knowing of her loss, they liked to share stories of similar loss.

"I'm so sorry."

"Are you going to stay?" Ruth asked.

"Yes, I'll be here for summer."

"I'm going to ask her to come and live with us on Cuttylea," Lottie continued. "But first everyone has to vote on it."

Killian figured everyone meant Elena and Ruth. She turned her attention back to the woman with the injured arm. "This is a very nice place. Peaceful. She might like it."

"How about after?" Ruth wanted to know. "After the summer."

Killian realized she was carrying on two separate conversations.

"After? I...I only have a job here for summer."

"So you think I should ask her?" Lottie pressed.

"Absolutely. Of course, the choice ultimately is hers. She can decide if she wants to come here or not. But I don't see why she wouldn't."

"So, you *are* staying." Lottie announced, smiling and reaching with her good hand to her sister.

Totally confused, Killian turned to Perth. He seemed amused by the exchange, too. He glanced at the door.

"It was really nice meeting you," she said. "I have to be on my way."

Ruth got up and walked them to the door and brushed a kiss on Perth's cheek.

"Now, you make sure to bring your girl back here for a visit."

Killian knew there was no point in reminding them that she worked at the inn and that she was here more than Perth.

"They're very sweet and totally senile," he whispered after the apartment door closed and they were on their way downstairs. "Lottie took a tumble this afternoon. It's uncertain whether the cat or the carpet is to blame. But they'll be arguing about it for the next five years or so."

"Are you the only doctor on this island?"

"Not doctor. I'm the fix everything sugar pill."

"Right." Killian knew firsthand that he was just being modest. She hadn't forgotten her fall from the cliffs at the tower and what he'd done to 'fix' her.

The voices of Liz and Amanda drifted up from the kitchen.

"Are you leaving now?" he asked.

"After I drop this basket off."

"I'll wait for you outside," he said, brushing his fingers against hers and going out the main door, bypassing the kitchen.

Putting the basket back in a supply closet downstairs, Killian's hope of a quick exit ended when Amanda cut off her escape.

"Hey, Brittany's birthday is Friday. They're throwing a surprise party for her at our house. I'd really like you to come."

The party was four days off. It was difficult to come up with an excuse not to go.

"Liz has already mentioned it to Perth," Amanda persisted. "He's going."

"Okay. Thanks."

She'd go. But she might have a difficult time not tearing out Brittany's golden hair. Just let the birthday girl try pawing Perth.

Killian went out, and a blanket of stars melting into a black sea greeted her. The night air was balmy with a soft, warm breeze. The sounds of the night surf overpowered the occasional voices drifting out from the windows of the dining room. A dozen steps down the grassy hill, she saw Perth's dark shadow, facing the sea. She walked toward him.

"No long distance swim tonight?"

He turned and stretched a hand in her direction. "I am going now. Come down to the beach with me."

Killian placed her hand in his, and they started down the hill.

"When is the next competition?"

"I don't know. I don't think I'm going."

She looked at him, surprised. "If you're worrying about Walt, I can help out while I'm here. I'm not positive, but I think he'd tolerate my company off and on for a day or two."

His thumb caressed the back of her hand. "I think he'd more than tolerate your company. He likes you."

"I wouldn't go that far."

"He asked me today to invite you over for dinner tomorrow night. Believe me, that's a first."

"A first time for him cooking?"

"No, a first time to invite anyone over. Neighbors and friends come and go, but never an invitation to a sit-down dinner."

"I hope you're not cooking," she said in a teasing tone.

He pulled her into a headlock.

"Okay. Okay. I'm coming. But I'm going to eat first before I come over."

They stopped at the bottom of the grassy hill. He stepped off a stone ledge onto the sand, and she followed. The beach here was protected by a stone jetty, but the waves were crashing in the distance.

His hands slipped around her waist and he drew her to him. His mouth closed on hers before she had any time to react.

Killian's mind emptied of everything but him and the burning shocks running through her body.

The voices of people up the hill brought them back to reality. Perth ended the kiss, but stood with his forehead against hers. Their eyes met in the darkness.

"I don't understand it," he said in a low voice.

"Me? Us?"

"Your effect on me."

She let her fingers trail upward to his face. She touched his lips.

"Is it so bad?"

He kissed her again, this time with more passion than she could handle, his hand roaming to her breast, down across her ribs to her belly.

Killian broke off the kiss and stepped back. She felt lightheaded. She was shaking.

"This is all new to me. I'm not...I've never..."

She turned and moved toward the dark water whispering on the soft sand of the beach. Killian was learning quickly that there were consequences in every decision she made. Not making peace with her stepmother over the past four years made her an outsider. Not applying to colleges in the last year of high school put her at the mercy of her father's whims. Going too far with Perth would make her vulnerable in ways that she wasn't prepared to face.

He came down the beach toward her. She looked over her shoulder. He'd discarded his shirt. He walked into the water until he was waist deep. He turned back to her.

"I have to swim. It has nothing to do with competitions or prizes. I need this. Every day. For hours at the time. The ocean draws me in. It's part of me. Like the air we breathe. Without the water, I know I'd die."

Killian stared. "I don't understand."

"You—somehow only you—fill the same need in me."

He turned and disappeared into the dark sea.

CHAPTER 19

"Was that Perth Jonson with you on the beach last night?"

Killian felt the hackles on her neck rise. She'd been the first one at work this morning, so Elena had asked her to deliver breakfast trays to the cottages. It was her bad luck that Davenport was the one waiting outside.

She put the two trays on the table and set up the napkins and silverware. She decided to ignore the question. "Is there anything else I can get for you this morning?"

"I need to meet with Perth." Davenport reached for his wallet.

She stepped down the porch. "Sorry, I can't help you."

"If you're any kind of friend of his, then you'd help me."

Killian picked up the other trays and started toward the other cottage. She wasn't going to stand there and argue with this man. Davenport had already met with Walt. Whatever he needed with Perth would have to happen through his father.

Thankfully, a couple of yawning researchers greeted her at the next cottage. Polite conversation and nothing more. The trouble was that she had to walk past the first cottage on her way back to the inn. Davenport was standing in the path, waiting.

"Look, I've left him a message with the innkeeper," he started. "His father is being irresponsible. Perth's life is in danger. Wouldn't you want to know if you had a rare blood disease that, untreated, could kill you any day?"

Killian stared past the researcher at the inn up the hill. Of course she would want to know. She felt Perth had the right to know, too. But her instincts were telling her to not trust this man. Walt loved his son. He wouldn't hurt him.

"I'm sure Elena will pass your message on to him."

She tried to go around him, but he managed to block her again.

"He's a distance swimmer. How would you feel if he had a stroke out in the ocean during one of his long swims?" he persisted. "Stroke and heart attack are common side effects of the disease. And they become more of a risk with any kind of extreme physical activity."

Killian doubted that was likely. People on the island trusted Perth's healing abilities. So did she. If he 'fixed' everyone else, couldn't he do the same thing for himself?

"He's a college kid. Have him look up JAK mutations on line. That's what his father has. I guarantee you that Perth has the same thing. Tell him that much. And tell him I'm here when he's ready to meet with me."

He stepped aside, and Killian hurried up the path to the inn.

There was no mention of 'JAK mutation' or 'JAK blood disorder' in the twenty-year-old encyclopedia on the inn's library shelves. Elena had no Internet access. Not even a dial-up hookup for her computer.

But Killian couldn't shake off Davenport's words.

With more people moving in today, Elena had set up a schedule where the three girls could split the work on different shifts. Killian offered to be the first one in every day. Amanda came in at ten o'clock, and Killian's shift ended at two in the afternoon. Brittany and Liz would be working the dinner shift.

Doing food prep in the kitchen right before lunch, Killian decided to pick Elena's brain about what she'd overheard a couple of nights ago.

"Perth's father has invited me over to their place for dinner tonight."

"That's wonderful," the innkeeper said, beaming.

"I don't really know him."

"He's Perth's father. That makes him a really good guy. That's all you need to know."

"Seriously, do you know anything about him before he came to the island? What he did for living? What his wife was like? It would be nice to know a little before I show up."

Elena poured a bottle of dressing on some cut-up vegetables and tossed them. Her gaze remained on the mixture in the bowl. "Well, as you noticed already, this is a pretty small island. Very few live here year round. Our tendency has always been to welcome people and not try to pry into their past."

"I wasn't exactly prying," Killian said defensively.

"I know, sweetie." She smiled. "I can tell you that Walt is a very private man. Whatever he wants to share of his past will have to come from him."

"At least, tell me one thing. Is he sick? Like...dying?"

Elena looked at her incredulously. "Dying? Oh, no. Other than being in wheelchair, Walt is as healthy as a horse. He's been that way as long as I've known him."

Killian cornered Amanda before leaving. "Do you have a way of checking email or getting on the Internet during the summer?"

"Sure," the young woman answered. "The house we rent has satellite for TV and Internet. It's really good connection, too. And thankfully, we don't have to pay for it. It comes with the rent."

"Could I come over some time and check my email?"

"Absolutely. All the summer kids do. When do you want to come over?"

Davenport's warnings continued to gnaw at her. She had to find out more about this before she saw Perth tonight.

"How about today? After you get out of work?"

"Sure. Come back at four, and we'll walk back to the house together."

"Sounds great."

As Killian was on her way out, Elena stopped her. She had an overnight mail packet in her hand. "I almost forgot to give this to you. It arrived this morning."

Killian looked at the sender's address. It was from her father. Adding to the aggravation of what was inside, he'd made a conscious decision to send it to the inn, rather than to Hannah's address. He wanted to make sure she got it. She stuffed it in her backpack and went out the door.

Standing in the bright afternoon sun, Killian looked out at the boats coming and going in the harbor. The ferry was just working its way into the dock. People were crowded along the railings. The summer population was definitely on the rise.

Descending the hill to the cluster of houses around the harbor, she spotted Eric standing by the ice cream shack. He waved and started toward her. She waved back but went in the opposite direction.

Killian was in no mood for company. She knew Perth must be working at the salt pond. Hannah was helping Daniel Sawyer with one of his civic duties. She couldn't even bring herself to pretend to be social. She was confused about everything in life, and there was no escape wherever she looked. She glanced over her shoulder. Eric was still coming after her.

At the end of the cluster of weathered cottages that comprised the island's 'downtown', Killian's eye was caught by a small sign next to the side door of a building containing a gallery for nautical art.

Cuttylea Island Historical Society
Hours: By Appointment

Killian tested the door. It opened. She slipped in and closed it behind her. Narrow stairs led to the second floor. At the bottom of the stairs, a sign with an arrow read, *Admission Free— Donations Appreciated*. Beneath it, a wooden box hung on the wall.

A sheer curtain covered a glass panel in the door, and Killian peered though it. A moment later, Eric went past the door. Almost immediately, she heard him speak to someone.

"Did you just see Killian? She should have gone by you."

"Nope. Maybe she went into one of the shops." She recognized the second voice as Josh.

"Help me look for her."

"Bullshit. I'm supposed to meet my cousin at the ferry. You're on your own, man."

Not so long ago, in another life back in a boarding school in Vermont, she was invisible to boys like these. But somehow on Cuttylea, everyone seemed to notice her. For this afternoon, anyway, she'd be happy having some of that anonymity back.

She reached into her pocket and found a dollar bill. She pushed the money into the box on the wall and headed upstairs.

The door at the top was open.

"Hello," she called out softly, receiving no answer.

Going in, Killian looked around at an open space beneath gabled roofs. Glass top tables and display cases contained artifacts and pictures. Glancing through one of the windows at the street, she saw Eric sitting on a dock piling by the water, waiting for her to reappear.

Killian decided this was as good a place as any to spend a couple of hours before getting back to the inn.

Starting at one wall, she perused a section filled with models and historical photos of work boats and sailing ships. There was a section devoted to the whaling history of the island. One case contained logbooks that dated back a couple of centuries. Another focused on ships that had been wrecked along the rocky coasts of the area islands. She looked up at an old map of Cuttylea Island, dated 1867, hanging on the wall. The sites where ships had gone down were clearly marked.

She searched for Squibnocket Point and the reef where Perth had saved those two boys' lives. There were five shipwrecks marked around that same spot.

Before moving away from the map, Killian's attention was drawn to a mark below the faded signature of the artist. A pentagram. She tried to read the name, but couldn't. Looking back up at the map, she noticed the same mark was repeated in pencil next to or below many houses. Hannah's cottage was one of them. Walt's house. And the inn. A larger pentagram marked the cemetery.

Backing away, Killian's gaze took in all the other artifacts in the room. A door at the corner farthest from the stairs drew her attention.

Killian walked to it and tested it. Like every other door on the island, it was unlocked.

A long, narrow workroom of sorts. No windows. The light from the larger room poured in. Killian saw that one wall was covered with old photographs. Some were framed individually. Other frames held groups of photos.

She tugged on a string hanging down from the ceiling, and a series of fluorescent lights sputtered and came to life.

At first glance, she didn't see any dates or names on the old black and white photos. Only images. Places on the island that looked so familiar. People long dead, she assumed. Looking at the style of clothing and the quality of photographs, Killian guessed some of these went back to the 1800s.

Killian moved from frame to frame, photo to photo. So many of the faces looked strangely familiar, regardless of the clothing. She found her great aunt Hannah in many of them. She didn't look much different than she did today.

On the end wall, large group photos had been arranged beneath a handmade sign decorated with calligraphy. *Fourth of July.*

Killian's breath caught in her chest. All of the pictures had been taken in the same place. The old stone Tower.

The black-and-white photograph at the very top depicted women in long skirts, men with old-fashioned moustaches and beards. They were all wearing hats and jackets. At the center of the photograph, a young couple was seated. The woman's eyes drew Killian in. The shape of the face was the same as her own. And the large young man looked very much like Perth.

Her heart pounded. Her gaze moved from one group portrait to the next. It was obvious the pictures had been arranged chronologically, but they were large gaps in time between them. Clothing styles changed. Occasionally, uniforms appeared. Some of the faces changed, aging. Some disappeared. New faces took their place. But the centerpiece of the photo always seemed the same--a young couple seated among the islanders. They were clearly a different couple in each photograph, but they always had an eerie similarity to Killian and Perth.

The last couple of pictures were in color. She recognized Hannah and Daniel Sawyer and Elena. Ruth and Lottie stood arm in arm. Other islanders looked familiar, as well.

At the center of the last group photograph, a rather unhappy looking young man was staring tensely at something in the distance. Gazing carefully at the image, she realized that he could easily be taken for Perth's brother. Beside him sat a young woman who was about the same age as Killian was now.

It was her mother Ama, smiling into the camera.

CHAPTER 20

The layout of Walt's cottage was similar to Hannah's, except that the addition of a couple of rooms in the back provided wheelchair-friendly living arrangements.

"Why don't you two be useful? Start the grill and then you can show Killian around," Walt told Perth. "Hannah can help me with the salad and the table."

Killian was happy to get away from the older people right now, even though she had been relieved to know that Hannah was coming to dinner at Walt's, too. She was having trouble keeping up a façade of cheerfulness.

She followed Perth out to a grassy area in back of the house and watched him empty a bag of charcoals into a built-in stone grill and light it.

He glanced at her. "What's wrong?"

She didn't know where to start.

Sea-green eyes met hers. His hand came up, a thumb gently caressing her cheek for a moment before dropping back to his side.

Troubles shifted and her priorities cleared in her mind.

"Do you know anything about a scientist--a doctor named Davenport--who's staying at the inn right now?"

"One of the wind farm people?"

"Yeah."

"Why?"

"Do you know anything more about him?"

He shook his head. "Why?"

"Elena or Walt didn't say anything about him?"

"No, why would they?"

Good or bad. Trust or not. Killian decided the decision had to be Perth's and no one else's.

"He wants to see you. Talk to you. He already spoke to your father and left a message for you at the inn."

"About what?"

"He claims…he says…he alleges…" Killian paused, feeling like one of those pharmaceutical ads with a dozen disclaimers running on a banner at the bottom of the TV screen. "Okay, let me start again."

She glanced toward the house making sure there was no sign of Hannah or Walt.

"Davenport was apparently Walt's doctor before your father moved to Cuttylea Island. A specialist."

"What kind of specialist?"

"According to Davenport, Walt had or has a rare and dangerous blood disorder. He called it a 'JAK mutation'. He claims you could be carrying the same thing without knowing it."

He stared at her in silence for a moment. Killian wished she could read his mind. She hadn't been with her mother the first time the doctors told her about the cancer. She would never know how Ama reacted. Killian had only been witness to her mother's bravery afterward, including the time when they'd told her there was no hope.

"Did this guy say anything more about it? What it is? How it might be affecting my father?" He was more concerned about Walt than himself.

She shook her head. "After work, I went with Amanda to the house she's renting. I looked it up on the Internet."

"What did it say?"

"It's really rare," she told him. "A JAK mutation or disorder causes the body to make too many red blood cells. These extra cells make the blood thicker than normal. Blood clots can form. And if a person is active, they can have a stroke. The mutation is inherited, but it's easily diagnosed with a blood test."

"Walt hasn't seen a doctor for as long as I can remember."

"Your father supposedly got a number of treatments of some experimental drug from Davenport before coming here. That might have fixed the problem. Also, he's confined in his wheelchair. Limited exercise."

She took his hand in hers, entwining their fingers. Emotions built up in her. She already cared so much for him. "You, on the other hand, are in danger."

He picked up a stick and poked a couple of times at the charcoal.

"Come on. Let me show you the inside."

He was dismissing the whole thing.

"Have you ever had a blood test?" Killian asked, walking with him back toward the house.

"No."

"Maybe you should think about it."

He nodded, obviously ready to change the topic. Killian figured she'd said her peace.

"Charcoals will be ready in half an hour," he told Walt, sticking his head into the kitchen before taking her hand and leading her up the narrow stairs.

A small landing on the second floor opened onto a bathroom and two bedrooms. She never had a chance to even look around before Perth pulled her into his arms and seared her lips with a kiss. She leaned into him, losing herself in his taste and touch. His hand moved down her back and gathered her so close against his body that there wasn't a breath of air between them. The thin material of the sundress did nothing to separate her from his heat.

She'd read it in books, heard it in movies, heard her mother say it. What if I had a day left to live? A week? Fear for his life was like gasoline on the fire of passion she was feeling.

"I wanted to do this from the first moment you walked into the house," he whispered in her ear.

She'd tried to look good, applying a little makeup and letting her hair down.

"I'm glad I have this effect on you."

"Not as glad as I am," he growled in her ear. Lifting Killian off her feet, he carried her a couple of steps into his bedroom.

Pushing one strap of the dress down over her shoulder, he pressed his lips to the skin.

His mouth was hot. She loved the sensation. Hannah and Walt's voice drifted up from the kitchen.

Perth ran his hands down over the curve of her bottom and pulled her closer against him. She could feel how aroused he was. Unlike last time, she wasn't scared. She didn't move away. Instead, she let the thrill race to her very center.

Taking Perth's face in her hands, Killian placed soft kisses on his chin, his cheeks, his nose, before rubbing their lips softly together. She could read so much in his eyes. Desire, emotion. He threaded his fingers into her hair, drew her close and deepened the kiss.

Finally, she tore her mouth away, hardly able to catch her breath. "They're downstairs. We...we should go down."

He reluctantly let her go and stepped away. "I need a minute."

Killian turned away, trying to slow down her own pounding heart. Her body tingled all over. Her skin was burned where his lips had touched.

He turned on the light in the room, and for the first time she saw the walls.

Maps. Nautical charts. Notes pinned all over them. Photos with writing and circles and arrows. Every inch of the walls was covered.

Killian turned around in amazement. She walked to one wall and touched the pieces of paper taped to a map. "What are these?"

"Corrections," he said over her shoulder. "The tides are strong along the channels. The coastline underwater is constantly changing. I mark major changes wherever I see them."

"Waiting for Thomas to pick me up at Hyannis, I saw a poster saying that National Oceanic something or other pays people for submitting corrections."

"Yeah, the NOAA." He shook his head. "Nothing I do is scientific. I don't use precision instruments. I do this only for me."

She looked around her again. Each map seemed to be different. "What kind of area does this cover?

He let out a breath. "From the Elizabeth Islands in the west to the tip of Cape Cod in the north and as far south as Nantucket."

Training for marathon swim events couldn't require this kind of detail. She noted how deep some of the marked sites were. He spent endless hours down there. She recalled his words. *The ocean draws me in. It's part of me. Like the air we breathe. Without the water, I know I'd die.*

He was standing next to her.

"What are you looking for?" she asked.

"I don't know. But it's there. Waiting for me."

"What do you mean?"

"I'm looking for a door. Or maybe my way out." He shrugged. "I guess I'll figure it out when I find it."

CHAPTER 21

A lecture. About sex. About protection. From Hannah.

"Oh my God," Killian whispered to herself. Some ten hours later, her face was still burning with embarrassment.

As she started down the path from the inn to the cottages, she took a deep breath and shook her head.

After dinner with Perth and Walt, Hannah wanted to talk about sex. True, Killian had lost her mother four years ago. True, she had no adult female role model in her life. But she wasn't an idiot. And to get that kind of speech from her ancient great aunt was way, way too awkward.

Killian had assured the older woman that, although she'd gone to an all-girl boarding school, the talk was not necessary. Sex education was covered in the curriculum. The most discomforting part of it was that Hannah clearly thought that Perth and Killian were having sex every moment they were out of her sight.

"Hey."

At the sound of Perth's voice behind her, Killian jumped, nearly dropping the breakfast trays.

"I was hoping to catch you on your way down," he told her.

His hair was wet. The damp shirt clung to him, showing his muscles in a way she didn't want to think about right now. She guessed he was just coming back from a swim. His expression was drawn. He looked tired, even upset. It took great deal of control not to put the trays down and go to him.

"Are you working at the inn today?" she asked instead.

He shook his head. "Would you mind taking me to this scientist? I want him to do the blood test."

She hesitated. "Did you talk to Walt about it?"

"No."

"Don't you think you should?"

"No," he said firmly. "I want to get it done."

Killian didn't know why she was feeling guilty, but she figured it had something to do with driving a wedge of distrust between the father and son. All of this would have been much easier if Walt had brought it up.

"Are you going to his cottage now?" he asked.

"Yeah, this is Davenport's breakfast." She hefted the tray higher on her shoulder and started down the hill.

"I can carry it for you."

"No. Thanks."

Like all other days, the scientist was waiting on the porch. At the sight of Perth, he immediately stood up and came down the steps.

Killian mumbled introductions.

"I'm so relieved you had the sense to come and see me," Davenport said exuberantly. "I want to take you back to Boston and--"

"No," Perth told him flatly. "I want the blood test done here."

The researcher looked as if he was going to argue. Then he simply shrugged.

"Okay. We can do that."

Killian put the food trays on the table. She didn't want to walk away and leave Perth there. She could feel his nervousness. And she didn't blame him.

"Let me take down some medical history."

"No," Perth said stubbornly. "Just the blood test. That's all we're doing."

Davenport actually glanced in Killian's direction for help. She didn't say a word. She understood Perth's attitude. There was no reason to talk about it unless he had the blood disorder.

"You must have questions about what this is all about. About potential treatment. Your options. About what your father has been...or was...struggling with."

"I'm here for one reason. And that's for a blood test." Perth clipped his words as if he were speaking to a child. "If we can't do that, then I'll be on my way."

Killian liked the attitude. It was nice to see that Davenport's bossiness would have no effect on Perth. In fact, it was almost enjoyable watching the man struggle to keep his temper. Clearly not a guy who was accustomed to being spoken to this way.

"Fine. I have blood test kits inside. Sit down. I'll get my stuff." The scientist disappeared through the door.

Perth didn't come up onto the porch and instead sat down on the steps. There was no breakfast order for the other cottage, so Killian sat down next to him. He was so tense.

"When my mother was sick, I knew and she knew there was something seriously wrong. She looked sick. She definitely didn't feel good. Walt seems great, and you're the healthiest person I've met in my life."

"It's not that."

"What is it?"

"I'm not crazy about getting stuck with a needle," he blurted.

Killian fought the urge to smile. She took his hand instead.

"Let me redirect your subconscious."

"Very funny."

"Did you have a terrible experience as a child? Something having to do with needles?"

"No."

"You just don't remember it."

"I'm serious. I've never had a needle stuck in me."

"You must have," she insisted. "Vaccinations when you were a kid."

"Nope."

"You needed it for school."

"I was home-schooled here on the island."

"How about college?" she asked.

"I told you. I don't live on campus."

She shook her head in disbelief. "Come on. You walk barefoot all over the island. You had to have a tetanus shot or two sometime."

"No. Never have."

Killian sensed they were being watched. She looked over her shoulder and found Davenport standing in the doorway, listening to their conversation. This guy annoyed her to no end.

"I think he's ready for you," she said.

Killian hung around, watched closely as the scientist swabbed the skin on Perth's arm. The smell of rubbing alcohol hung in the air. He stuck the needle in and took three vials of blood. It seemed like way too much, but she kept the comment to herself. After all his worrying, Perth watched the whole thing and didn't flinch even once.

"When will you have the results?" he asked, peeling off the gauze as soon as it was taped onto his arm.

"About a week," Davenport replied. "I'm telling you right now that I'm prepared to start my old study again if you test positive. I will get the necessary approvals to give you the same treatment that your father had. Of course, Walt has to do his part. He'll have to step up and show everyone that my research did work."

Perth made no commitment of any sort and motioned to Killian to come back to the main house with him.

"Pretty brave," she said when they were out of earshot.

"Thanks for waiting there with me."

"You're welcome. I think he's kind of a creep, to be honest."

He took her hand, stopping her before they reached the inn. "When is your day off?"

"Tomorrow."

"Any plans?"

"No," she said, hoping.

"Good. Spend it with me. There's a place I want to take you."

Killian didn't care where. There was no other place she wanted to be but with him. And she knew exactly how Hannah would feel about it, too. In spite of her lecture, she wanted the two of them together, morning, night, and every hour of the day.

"Let me know when you're ready tomorrow, and I'll meet you."

"I wanted to ask you, have you ever seen the photographs in the historical society?"

"No. Actually, I've never even been in there."

Killian was about to continue when she heard Liz's voice. " What are you doing here? Have you given up sleeping?"

"No more sleeping," Brittany replied brightly. "This is my 'week-before-my-birthday' resolution. I'm not spending an extra minute in bed unless he's in there with me. So where is he?"

"He went down toward the cottages a while ago."

Brittany and Liz were standing just inside the screen door to the kitchen. They hadn't seen the two of them coming up the hill. Killian looked at Perth, and he frowned.

"Wish me luck."

The screen door squeaked open.

"Hey!" Brittany chirped, coming out of the inn.

The pale yellow sundress showed enough skin to stop traffic. As she came down the steps, she ran a serious risk of bouncing right out of the halter top.

"I've been looking all over for you."

Brittany brushed past her, never even acknowledging that she was there. Perth made some polite comment. Killian started up the steps.

"You promised to coach me, don't forget. Today's the day."

"Look, I've got a lot of—"

"I even brought my suit."

Killian looked back. Brittany was waving the tiniest string bikini top this side of St. Bart's.

"You just have to promise not to look when I change into it," Brittany said coyly.

Resentment at being dumped was not an unfamiliar feeling. Her father's relationship with his new family had anchored it right beneath Killian's skin. What was running hot in her veins right now was different. She was angry about this skank thinking she could throw herself at Perth. She'd never seen him give Brittany any encouragement. But she was always turning up. Always pushing.

Opening the screen door, Killian looked down the hill and saw them going toward the beach. Brittany had linked her arm in his. The sound of her fake laughter reached her even here.

She banged the tray against her leg and went into the inn.

Great, she thought. Now she was jealous.

CHAPTER 22

"I'll splatter like a soft-boiled egg on those rocks."

"You won't. You'll be perfectly fine."

"There has to be another way to get down to the cave."

Killian looked down at the sheer cliff and the angry waters washing over the sharp rocks.

"It's easy. We just jump into the pool and go into the cave while the tide is still low. It's much more dangerous climbing down."

The so-called pool was just a distant speck below them. She shook her head and took half a step back. Her back came in contact with Perth's bare chest. His arms closed around her, entrapping her in his arms.

"Come on, Killian. This is nothing compared to the cliff by the Tower."

The feeling coursing through her definitely wasn't the 'spend-the-day-with-me' bliss she had imagined. Meeting him in front of Hannah's cottage, they'd walked through the woods to a part of the island she had never visited.

"And you know I won't let anything happen to you."

The trees behind them were tall and came almost to the cliff's edge. From here, she had no view of the Tower. In fact, as they walked together, Killian had no idea they were near the shore until she was suddenly looking down at the water.

Trying to get her bearings, she looked to the left and realized that the Squibnocket reef lay to their left. Beyond it, she could just make out the top of the lighthouse.

"Shoes off. Clothes off. Unless you want them all wet."

"No. Why is it so important for me to see this place, anyway?" she asked, trying to pry his fingers off her waist. He wasn't budging.

"I told you. The painting on the cave walls might answer some of your questions."

Killian shook her head again. "Look, only a crazy person would jump down there. On top of that, you have to be clinically insane or on a lot of drugs to go down there and paint stuff on cave walls that no one will see. I have no interest in seeing some Neanderthal idiot's graffiti."

"So you're going in with all your clothes on?"

She tried to extricate herself, but his arms were like steel bands around her.

"I really don't have any questions. It's all good. Let's go to the salt pond. You keep promising swim lessons."

"Too late. We're here. You are going to see this, one way or another."

Perth turned her in his arms. She looked up into his stubborn green eyes. She already knew the expression. He was going to take her down there kicking and screaming if he had to.

"Okay. You win. But give me a little space, big boy."

A smile tugged at his lips. His arms dropped to his sides. With the cliff edge behind her and his body in front, she didn't have much space to maneuver.

She kicked off her shoes and dropped the backpack on the ground. Quickly peeling off her tee-shirt, she reached down to undo her shorts. His eyes were on her bikini top, and Killian used the opportunity to shove at his chest, trying to escape.

Like a rock, he didn't budge. Instead, he pulled her against him and kissed her. A second later, they were airborne.

No free fall or rollercoaster could top the feeling in Killian's stomach. She screamed the entire time until they hit the water. No shattering on the rocks. No breaking into a million pieces. No transformation into a first course of soft-boiled eggs on a breakfast dish.

Perth never let her hand go. And as quickly as they shot downward into the pool, they were back to the surface.

Clutching at his neck, Killian gasped for air, tasting the salt water on her lips. She dashed her hair out of her face with one hand and looked up at the distance they had fallen. From here, she could see rocks protruding from the cliff walls. The pool was even smaller than it looked from above. And she was stunned to think that they'd hit the mark.

"That wasn't so bad, was it? Come on."

Giving her no time to answer. He climbed up onto the rocks, pulling her up behind him. He led her over the tops of rocks along the base of the cliff until they reached another, shallower pool.

"You have a thing or two to learn about taking girls on a date," she said, following him.

"I have a confession. This is not a date."

She didn't have time to be offended. They were standing at the low opening of a cave at the end of the pool.

"This is educational."

The top of the cave entrance was only about two feet above the surface of the water. Thoughts of being trapped as the tide came in ran through her mind.

"You're kidding."

Perth's hand never let go of hers. They waded through waist-deep water and entered the murkiness of the cave. The cold salt smell of wet rock and the sea assaulted her senses. Gurgling sounds echoed off the walls. Shining rivulets ran down the walls from a cave ceiling that was impossible to see in the dark. The distant sound of bats flapping their wings reached her ears.

"Did I tell you dark, wet, enclosed spaces are third on the list of things I'm not crazy about?"

"I know water is first. What's second?"

"Lightning."

The whites of his teeth flashed as he looked over his shoulder at her.

"What's funny?" she asked.

"Nothing. I'm just glad I'm not in the top three."

"Don't get too comfortable. You're in the top five and climbing. One more cliff dive into pools the size of a teacup could do it."

He squeezed her fingers and pulled her along. "I can live with that."

The water grew shallower as they moved over a surface of shifting sand and rocks. The air became thicker, the light dimmer. They were moving deeper into the bowels of the island.

"Hey!" Killian yelped, feeling some slimy creature slip by her leg. "I'm serious. I don't like this. Let's get out of here."

"We're almost there."

A moment later, they reached a sharp incline and suddenly she was standing on a stony ledge in almost complete darkness. Killian's eyes struggled to adjust. Looking back, a mere sliver of light stretched across the smooth water from the cave's entrance far behind them.

He let go of her hand, and Killian tried to not panic.

"You're not going anywhere," she warned.

She heard him bang a solid object a couple of times against the ground, causing an echo to reverberate from far away. Suddenly, the thin beam of a penlight streamed into the darkness.

"Waterproof," he explained, shining it up at his own face.

"Clever."

"Take a look at this."

Perth directed the light at a cave wall not ten feet from where they were standing. It was not graffiti, she realized. It was a real cave painting. And it was old. Really old.

"The painting sort of starts down there," Perth said in a low voice, shining the light toward one end of the wall before handing the flashlight to her.

Killian took it and moved toward the sloping stone wall.

"This is incredible," she murmured. Perth said nothing, but she could feel him behind her. Half of the painting consisted of the sea and its creatures. Fish and seals and whales filled the waters.

As she studied the painting, her eyes were drawn to the depiction of the shoreline. Stylized human stick figures were standing together, some in the water and some on dry land.

Farther along, she saw a depiction of a village. Huts surrounded a longhouse, and fish and skins of seals were drying on racks by fires. A group of natives--all women--stood in the center of the village.

Killian gazed at the images. A tall man stood near the group. The islanders were pushing a young woman toward him.

Killian stepped closer and stared. Above her, clearly painted on the stone, was a pentagram.

"There's more," Perth said from behind.

At one edge of the village, a hut stood apart from the others. Above it, there was again the sign of the pentagram.

Around the hut, islanders were dancing. Clearly visible inside, two figures were having sex.

As she stared at the picture, the words of old Lynx echoed in her head.

They're using you.

Killian's hand trembled and she touched the wall. The pentagram. The woman in the village and the one in the hut were the same. She was an offering.

The flashlight dropped from her fingers and hit the ground with an echoing boom before going out. She took a step back and came in contact with Perth. She jumped.

"What's wrong?"

"I want to leave."

"Killian."

He took her arm, but she shook off his touch and charged to the water's edge. The walls of the cave were closing in on her. There wasn't enough air. She trusted the people on this island. What if Lynx was right and she was only being used for some weird human sacrifice?

She splashed into the water and fell. Panicking, she pushed herself to her feet again, wading as fast as she could toward the slit of light. She fell again, and her mouth and nose filled with the salty brine.

Killian gasped when Perth suddenly had a hold on her arms and yanked her above the surface.

"What are you running away from?"

She stared up into his face in the semidarkness of the cave. Her heart was racing. Her feet still trying to move toward the entrance.

"Are you running away from *me*?"

Even in the murky light, she could see the hurt in his face.

"No. From that." She motioned with her head toward the walls. "Please. Get me out of here."

CHAPTER 23

The noisy, brightly lit beach house offered a blazing contradiction to the darkened cottages of the sleepy island village.

Standing on the winding lane and looking into the house, Killian could already tell this party scene was like many she'd seen in high school. Cranked up music, drinking, a whiff of pungent smoke, boys and girls locked in each other's arms in every corner, inside and out. Always an observer but rarely a partaker, she knew tonight would be the same. She'd walk through, pretend to make small talk, and escape at the first opportunity to her own corner of the world.

She just needed to make an appearance for Amanda.

No one noticed Killian when she entered the large beach house. She knew the layout of the place. She'd come here earlier in the week to get on the Internet about Walt's disease. Spacious and comfortable, it was obviously only used as a summer rental property and not as a home. The house had definitely seen better days. Regardless, she cringed at the sight of the bottles and cans piled everywhere. In the living room, it looked like a gallon of something had been spilled on the rug, and some joker had marked off the area like a toxic waste site. Two girls in high heels were dancing on a sofa like strippers, entertaining a group of drunken young men. In a nearby game room, more loud partiers were engaged in a dart game, but driving the darts into the paneled wall brought more cheers and laughter than hitting the cork target.

Bits and pieces of different conversations flooded Killian's ears.

"Only two kegs left…"

"Where is that skank we came in with?"

"Gene has the rum on the boat. I love that boat, man."

"…in the kitchen making drinks."

"Who could we send to the mainland tomorrow?"

"I need air. Where's the birthday girl?"

"Out on the beach with her boy toy."

Killian looked up. Liz was upstairs, leaning over the banister and talking to a couple standing on the stairs.

"You know how Brittany gets when she sets her mind on something."

Getting bumped from behind as a new group of guests stumbled in from outside; Killian made a beeline for the kitchen. She was relieved to find Amanda there emptying bags of chips into baskets. By the sink, a young man was standing behind an island, pretending to tend bar for a steady stream of customers.

"You came," Amanda said, looking almost relieved.

"This is a lot of people."

"Tell me about it. We're going to run out of food and booze in no time."

"I'm confused. Where did they all come from? They aren't working on the island for the summer, are they?"

Amanda smiled and shook her head. "A boat load of Brittany's friends came out for the weekend. Didn't I tell you? Yeah, her birthday is like a national holiday. Come on, give me a hand."

Killian picked up two baskets of chips and followed her friend out to the back porch. There were as many people out there as she'd seen inside.

"By the way, Perth is here."

She knew he was coming. She'd overheard Liz and Brittany talk about it at work. She was surprised, though, that Amanda realized that it mattered to her to know. The island was small. The summer help had to talk. Killian and Perth spent enough time together for everyone to notice. Still, it didn't seem to matter at all to Brittany.

They never had a chance to put the food down. The baskets were snatched away by the partiers.

"What do you say? Moonlight, beach? I brought a blanket. Wanna know my birthday wish?"

Killian recognized Brittany's voice, whiny and even louder than normal. She glanced at the groups and the couples hanging on the porch rail. Looking past them at the moonlit beach below, she saw them. She'd know his silhouette anywhere.

And Brittany was making certain everyone could hear her. She had her hands looped around his waist, pressing their bodies together.

"How long have we known each other?" she said. "Two, three years? I've been coming on to you forever. Come on, Perth. Right here on the beach. I'm all yours. Let's do it."

A sharp pain ripped through Killian's middle. Her vision blurred with the sudden threat of tears. The primitive images on the walls of the cave rushed into her brain. Sexual. Scary. In a way sacrificial.

Killian hated to admit it, but she knew how Brittany felt. Perth had it all. If it weren't for those images, she would have made love with him yesterday right in that cave. Or on the beach. She would at least have gone as far as he wanted. But after seeing the cave painting, she'd felt sheer panic. She had to get out of there. To get back to someplace safe. She didn't want to be used. And he'd complied.

But that had been the end of their day together. Maybe the end of everything.

She knew he was ready to take their relationship to the next step. But she'd backed out on him.

Now he had a willing partner. Killian had already been replaced.

She turned around and bolted inside the house.

"Killian," Amanda called after her.

She didn't stop, but hurried to the front door. More people were coming in. There was loud laughter, greetings. She shouldn't have come. She didn't belong. She wasn't like these people. She wasn't like anyone her own age. She was a reject. A loner.

By the time she made her way through the door, her emotions betrayed her. Tears ran down her cheeks.

Suddenly, someone grabbed her hand from behind, spinning her around.

"Hey, where are you going?"

Eric.

"I have to get back."

Killian was glad it was dark. She used her free hand and stabbed away the tears.

"Come on. This party is just starting." He took a step back, pulling her off balance. She fell against him. "Well, hi."

He smelled of alcohol and smoke. The party had been going strong for him for a while.

"I'm ready to go home."

"No. No. No. You can't go home yet. It's way too early." He pulled her hand under his arm and escorted her to a group of people by the side of the house. Josh was pouring shots of tequila on an end table they'd dragged outside.

"Well, what do you know?" Josh said, holding up two plastic cups to them. "The elusive Miss K makes an appearance. Where's the paparazzi when you need them?"

Eric took a cup and lifted it to her lips.

She turned her face away. "No. No thanks."

He shrugged, downed it, and reached for the other, but Josh had already hammered that one down.

Killian tried to free her hand, but he had her trapped. She told herself there was no reason to panic. There were plenty of people around. Most seemed oblivious to anything or anyone around them, but nothing was going to happen.

"I have to go. I have to be at work tomorrow at 8:00."

"Why do you always play so hard to get?" Eric asked.

The kicked puppy look, the wry smile, the mussed hair, the handsome face. He didn't look like a bad guy. He definitely didn't look dangerous.

"I don't know what you mean."

Holding her arm tightly, he started pulling her toward the beach. She dug in her feet.

"See what I mean? I only want to talk to you. Just take a walk and talk to you. Nothing more. And you're trying to run away."

Her emotions were raw enough, the pressure powerful enough, that she thought her head would explode. She didn't want to go anywhere with Eric, but she didn't want to make a scene, either.

"Okay, just talk," she told him.

He smiled and they started walking.

"Have fun, lovebirds," Josh called after them.

The party had spilled out beyond the porch onto the grass and down onto the beach. There were kids everywhere she looked.

"So what's up with you and that swimmer boy? Are you two going out?"

Before she could answer, a couple near them jumped up and ran toward the water, shedding clothes as they ran. They were naked before they splashed into the sea.

"So, are you?" Eric asked again.

"No," she said.

"Right answer," he said. "Considering the show he and Brittany are putting on right now hooking up on the beach."

Killian stopped dead in her tracks. She felt sick. "I really need to go back."

She tried to pull her hand away, but he held on to her tighter.

"What's wrong? You don't like watching other people have sex?"

"I don't want to talk about it."

"I don't like talking about it, either. Or watching. But I like doing it."

"Good for you," she said sharply. "Now, let go. Hannah is expecting—"

Intentional or accidental, she couldn't tell. But he stumbled and dragged her to the ground with him. The blades of grass were cool and sharp.

"Oh, sorry. I guess I might have had one too many. I'm not usually so clumsy."

She quickly pushed to her feet and wiped her wet palms on her shorts.

"Help me up?" He stretched out a hand.

Out of reflex, she reached down to help him, but when he grasped her hand she knew it was a mistake. A second later, she was sitting on his lap.

"Eric, let me go. I don't want to do this," she snapped, realizing his arms were already tight around her waist. She didn't want this. Thoughts of Perth coursed through her mind. No matter what was happening on the beach, he was the only one she wanted. The only one she wanted to be with.

"Have I told you how hot you are?"

"Eric. Seriously. No!"

There was nothing clumsy about the way he moved now, rolling her back onto the grass and moving on top of her. His mouth closed over hers. The kiss was rough and greedy. But before Killian could put up a real struggle, Eric's entire frame was yanked off of hers and thrown to the side. She heard the smack of a fist finding its mark.

"Fight!" someone shouted from the porch, eliciting echoes from inside the house. Immediately, partiers came running.

The two dark figures thrashed at each other, and Killian scrambled to her feet.

People hurried toward them from every direction. To her left, a group moved in, blocking her view of the two fighters. She shoved through to the center. Eric was on all fours, struggling to get up. Blood was dripping from his nose.

Perth stood a couple of steps away, hands clenched into fists. Ready to deliver the next punch.

Eric was panting. "Hey, dude. Stop. What the f—?"

She rushed inside the circle. As she did, Perth turned and Eric rose and dove toward him. Perth struck him again across the face, knocking him back to the ground.

"No. Please. No," Killian cried out, rushing between them.

Perth looked wild, dangerous. His eyes were focused on his opponent. She took hold of his wrists.

"Please, take him inside," she pleaded with the crowd around them.

A couple of the guys hurried to Eric. Perth took a threatening step toward them.

She held on to him. "That's enough. Please. *Enough*."

His gaze turned on her. There was an instant change. He seemed to see her for the first time.

"He was hurting you."

"I'm okay."

With the exception of the two helping Eric to his feet, everyone else continued to gawk at them in silence.

"Let's get out of here." She pulled on his hand. "Please."

Killian was relieved when he walked away with her. They left behind the crowd and the house. The hushed conversations followed them.

"Who was that?"

"Where did he come from?"

"I saw him run up from the beach."

"Look. Don't touch. That should teach Eric a lesson."

Killian didn't care where they went, so long as they were far from that party. Perth led the way. Neither said a word until they were standing on the quiet stretch of the beach in front of the inn.

Killian spoke first. "I appreciate what you were trying to do for me back there. But beating Eric up wasn't the answer."

"I had to get his attention."

"Why?" She looked up at him, confused. "Why would you care? You were with Brittany on the beach. Hooking up. That was the talk of the party."

"And you believed them?"

And then he kissed her. A hungry crush of lips and tongue.

Backing away from her, he peeled the shirt off his back and tossed it on the sand. She watched him stride to the water and wash the blood off his knuckles.

"You're the one, Killian," he said, rising and looking back at her. "The one in my head. I can't shake you. I couldn't be with someone else and not feel guilty about how bad you would feel. I don't know why, but I can't."

Killian's feet were cemented to the sand. Her heartbeat drumming in her ears. But she wasn't fooled. This wasn't some sweet declaration of affection or love. She heard, woven into his tone, resentment.

"I didn't call you. I didn't ask for your help. And I didn't plant myself in your head." She stopped.

A deep, drawn out booming sound was rising from the sea. Almost a roar. Like a prolonged movement deep in the ground.

"What was that?" she murmured.

Perth turned around, staring out at the night sea. Beyond him, a flash of lightning in the distance outlined his silhouette.

Killian felt the sand under her feet begin to shift. She looked down, feeling the vibrations.

"Is it an earthquake? A tsunami?"

And then, as suddenly as it began, it was over. The ground she stood on became still. Silence filled the darkness once again.

When she looked up, Perth was gone.

CHAPTER 24

The intermittent gusts of wind were enough to ruin her sleep, but the dull thud of the walking stick and the shuffling of feet on the lane had to be a nightmare.

Killian rolled over and pulled the pillow over her head. She hated this limbo-like state, not knowing if she was conscious or dreaming, not knowing if she was awake or asleep. She hated hovering where she was, over the blurred line between reality and fantasy.

The shuffling continued. She was awake. He was in the lane by Hannah's cottage. She didn't have to see him. Lynx wouldn't leave her alone. The strange man's warnings were a continuous harassment.

At the sharp knock on the door, Killian bolted upright in bed. There was a moment of silence before she heard Hannah hurrying down the stairs. The kitchen door creaked open.

What do you want? What are you doing here?

Keep her away.

Hush! She might hear you.

She won't fare well if you don't keep her away.

Killian recognized Lynx's raspy voice. A double flash of lightning lit her room, and a low rumble of thunder followed. She stood up and quietly went to the bedroom door. She didn't open it, thinking of the squeaky hinges.

You're talking nonsense. And you know the rules. You don't come to the village. Not like this.

Killian had been told Lynx didn't talk. Another lie. It was obvious Hannah had no trouble communicating with him, either.

They're coming for him.

That can't be so. Hannah's voice rang with concern. *It's too soon.*

The blue hole is starting to open.

Does Perth know? Hannah asked in a worried tone.

He might. If not, he'll know soon enough.

I have to get everyone together. They should all be told. You go back.

His voice took on a threatening tone. *Send her away. She must go back to her own people.*

No. We'll let fate take its course.

Don't play the fool. It will not happen. They won't allow it.

It's not their decision to make. It's Perth's.

They've trusted you with their own. Once again, you're trying to break a promise.

I'm doing no such thing. Perth will make the choice.

A gust of wind hammered at the house, causing them to pause. Killian looked at her window. All night, distant lightning had accompanied the wind gust, and yet there was no rain. Diamond stars continued to glimmer in the black velvet sky over the island.

What you are doing is wrong. You know it.

This is no different than what we've done for ever. For as long as I can remember. Hannah's voice rang out louder. Her confidence more pronounced. *No different than we've done for centuries.*

There was never such a chance of ruin before. This time he might choose her.

Then it's meant to be.

And you think that will be the end of it?

Go back to your side of the island. You delivered the message. Your job is done. I have to get ready.

Killian's heart pounded in her ears. Her throat felt dry. Fear, shock, confusion, all blended, bringing a numbing sense of helplessness. The graves of her ancestors in the cemetery, all dying young. The mark of the pentagram on her own body. The painting on the cave wall. The questions wouldn't stop.

But where was she to go? Who could she ask for help? What were they going to do to her?

She had to find Perth. This involved him as much as her. Perhaps more. This blue hole, wherever that was, clearly concerned him. Someone was coming for him.

She thought of the noise she heard on the beach tonight. The shifting of the sand. Perhaps it was a sign of what Lynx was talking about.

On wobbly legs, Killian made her way to the window and watched Lynx make his way slowly up the lane toward the woods. A ghoul in the night. A harbinger of doom.

Seconds later, she heard the door again open and close downstairs. Hannah was going toward Walt's place. She paused once and looked back at the cottage. Killian stepped back into the shadows of her bedroom as her great aunt gazed up at her window. Then she turned and hurried to Walt's house. As Hannah moved up the ramp, a gust of wind whipped her shawl around her.

She rapped on the screen door. A moment later, Killian heard her voice.

"Walt, Lynx brought news. The blue hole is opening. I need to spread the word. We'll meet at the Tower."

A muffled answer came from the house. Without another word, Hannah turned and went down the lane toward the harbor.

Trying to put on some clothes, Killian felt like she was moving in slow motion. Her hands and feet didn't belong to her. She lacked control. The strangeness of everything that was happening just shut down her ability to think and act. It was a waking nightmare.

She was still not dressed when she heard footsteps on the lane. As she looked out, flashes of lightning illuminated faces she knew. Islanders. People who lived here year around. Thomas Eliot. Elena. The innkeeper's old mother and aunt, moving right along as if they were not affected at all by their advancing years. Next door, Walt's wheelchair came down the ramp and joined the line going toward the woods. Toward the Tower.

Killian hurried downstairs. She slipped out the kitchen door and hid in the shadows of the house. There was no sign of Perth. As far as she knew, he was still swimming.

The numbers were thinning. Those trailing the procession were hurrying to catch up. She made up her mind. There was no place she could run to. She recalled the photos she'd seen in the upstairs room of the historical society. Her mother. Her grandmother. Others in her family had faced the same moment. All those women had spent time among these islanders.

Her mother always spoke with great fondness of her summers here. There was no hint of fear in those memories. Ama had left the island and married and had a child. No one had hurt her. No one would hurt Killian. They wouldn't force her do anything against her will. Hannah had even said so back in the cemetery. The choice lay with her.

Daniel Sawyer hurried past the cottage. He appeared to be the last person coming up the hill. Killian stayed in the shadows until the man went by. Then she followed.

They were going to the Tower. That much she knew. But getting there was another thing. Walt had told her the first night she'd met him that there was a shorter route, but Killian didn't know it.

When she entered the woods, the darkness became ominous. Around her and above her, gusts of wind came out of nowhere, whipping the treetops and grinding branches together. The damp smell of the deep woods rose up, making her shiver even as she walked.

Killian didn't dare turn on the flashlight she brought along. She didn't want to get caught. Not far away, she heard Daniel cough. He was moving away from her. A flash of lightning showed no fork in sight. He'd left the path, but there was no sign of a route. She waited, listening.

Killian shivered as whispers came to her. Beyond the rustle of leaves on trees, the cry of an owl in the night, the wind...voices came to her. Snatches of conversation coming from every direction.

How long?
We're not supposed to keep him.
The legend says we can try.
How long?
An old woman's voice. *The last time it took days.*
The door will open.
He goes through... never seen again.
And people die.
How quickly?
Hours. Not days. Hours.
Who tells him?

Killian jumped at the sound of a branch snapping behind her. She pressed her back against the trunk of a large tree and waited.

Three dark figures came into view. As they drew near, Killian recognized them. One was the woman who ran the ice cream stand at the dock. They carried no flashlight. No slowing down.

Killian panicked.

They stopped by a thicket of evergreen trees a few steps from her. Killian held her breath.

The three islanders did not hesitate. They knew exactly where they were headed. Pushing through the branches between a pair of pines, they left the path and disappeared.

Killian stepped out of the shadows. The branches had fallen back in place, forming a thick, unbroken line of green. She pushed through. A wide path lay right past it. She followed.

Keeping track of the voices, she let the sounds lead her through the dark.

Ten minutes she walked. Fifteen. Not much more, she was certain. As the trees thinned out, flashes of lightning brightened the sky. Crossing meadows, the more frequent gusts of wind pushed at her, whipping the hair around her face.

Suddenly, the Tower rose ahead of her. Seeing the islanders gathered at the base of the stone structure, she stopped. Away from the village, their concern about being discovered was discarded.

So who tells Perth?

Walt.

What is there to hold him here?

A long pause, then Elena's voice.

Walt. Us. The only people he's ever known as family. The graves up in the cemetery. Hannah has to tell him what's at stake.

Killian watched from the edge of the clearing as the islanders went into the Tower. The sound of their voices lessened until she could not hear them at all. She contemplated what to do.

The touch on her bare shoulder was cold, damp. It was the hand of Death. Killian gasped and jumped away. Lynx.

The old man's hand slowly dropped to his side. His face was in shadow, but his sightless eyes glowed.

"You cannot let them use you."

She stepped back.

"They're meddling with power beyond their understanding."

Killian continued to back away.

"You are the only one who will suffer."

"I don't know what you're talking about. I don't understand any of this." Killian walked backward toward the tower. He matched her steps, following her.

"You will suffer. You will be punished. And for nothing."

She turned around and ran. Reaching the Tower, she glanced back. He was still there, his stick raised like some evil wizard. She slipped inside the door of the Tower.

Killian looked around. They were all there on the ground floor. The entire village. The circle closed around her.

There was no escaping.

"You're here," Hannah said, coming toward her. "We were waiting for you."

CHAPTER 25

Killian stepped into the center of their circle. Someone had relit the fire she and Perth found the first day she came to the Tower. The growing flames hissed and popped, throwing off devilish shadows that danced wildly on the stone walls.

She thought of the pentagram floor directly above. They'd expected she would come. This was part of their plan.

Lynx prowled the woods outside. The islanders lay in wait inside. She didn't know who was more dangerous.

"What's this about?" she asked, turning to the faces lit up by the flames. "Why are you all here?"

No one answered. They were holding on to the pretense of being kind souls that she could trust.

Killian turned to the one person on the island who claimed, at least, to be family.

"Hannah, please. No more lies. Tell me what this is all about."

The old woman looked around the room as if considering how to respond. Killian had no time to waste. She turned to Perth's father.

"You've been the most honest of all of them. I hear things. The conversations. I know what Lynx said when he showed up at Hannah's door tonight. I already know this involves Perth more than it concerns me. You're his father. Please, Walt."

"Perth isn't my son."

Hannah put a hand on Walt's shoulder, stopping him from saying more.

Killian stared for a moment, then realized that she'd hoped for this. After hearing Davenport, after learning of Walt's life-threatening blood disorder, she'd wished deep down that this was so. She looked at her aunt.

"I'm not going to ask what else you've lied about," Killian said curtly. "I'm more interested in knowing if anything that I've seen or heard on this island is true."

"You *are* my great niece," Hannah said softly. "Not directly by blood. But you are the descendent of my half-sister, Hazel Ama Winthrop."

If Hazel was her grandmother or great-grandmother or something else, Killian had no idea.

"Why did you bring me to Cuttylea?"

Elena stepped forward and spoke. "Because you are part of this," the innkeeper said. "The legend. Everything."

"What do you mean? What legend?"

"The legend of Persus, the sea king's son, and Ama, the princess born with the mark of the pentagram."

"Perseus? Like in Greek mythology?"

"No, this Persus predates any Greek god," Hannah explained. "And what we know and share with you today isn't anything you'll find in any school book. This belongs to the island."

"Nothing has ever been written about it," Lottie chirped in. Killian looked at her, standing with her sister.

"And we've always made certain that nothing would be," Ruth added with a note of sternness. "This is our history. Our secret."

If that was a threat, Killian decided not to respond to it. She was more interested in keeping them talking about this legend.

"Long ago, before colonists came across the Atlantic," Hannah said, "Cuttylea Island was blessed with a special gift. The native people here were what we now call Cherokee. Ama was one of them."

"We've raised the Aquarians' chosen son for centuries," Lottie said.

"Aquarians?" Killian asked, confused.

"People who come to us from the sea," Elena explained. "For generations, they have brought us a chosen infant son. We raise him. And then he goes back to sea. Then, after a few years, a new child is brought to us. Perth came to us this way."

"Perth is an Aquarian," Hannah said quietly.

"Wait. This is insane," Killian replied. "You're telling me people actually walked out of the water and handed you Perth?"

Hannah shook her head. "No. That's why Lynx is here. It is his purpose. He is the guardian. The keeper of secrets. And he has been here on the island for longer than any of us in this room remember. Lynx was put here to watch over the child. He gives us the infant. He tells us when the sea door is about to open. The time when the Aquarian must leave. The old man is one of them."

Lynx and his strangeness. Lynx threatening Killian to go away. Lynx arriving at the village tonight, bringing news of a blue hole having arrived.

"This sea door. It's the blue hole."

"Yes," Elena replied. "The blue hole. An underwater cave. The door to their world."

Questions were piling up in her brain, but Killian forced them back.

"There's more to this," the innkeeper continued. "In return for our help, we receive something very special. While the child, the Aquarian, lives among us, no one dies on Cuttylea."

Killian tried to take this in. She thought of the photographs on the wall. Of her seemingly ageless great aunt. Of the dates on the gravestones in the cemetery.

"And it's not only that we continue to live so long, dear," Lottie broke in. "There is healing, too. Perth can fix people. Bones heal instantly. Cancer disappears. Pain goes away. There's no physical suffering here on the island. You just ask Walt."

Killian looked at him. He was staring at his hands. In another lifetime, she would have thought all of this was nonsense. But not now. Not here. Not after what she'd gone through herself. Not after all the strange things she'd witnessed.

"What's my part in this? My mother's part?" Killian asked. "I saw the photographs at the historical society. In every picture, there was always one of them, an Aquarian, someone looking like Perth. And a young woman that I'm guessing is one of my ancestors."

"This is where legend finds its roots," Elena responded.

Others spoke up.

"Never proven."

"But not too farfetched."

"It could be true."

"We believe it is true," Ruth immediately corrected.

Many of the islanders were talking at the same time. Killian stood and listened, taking the information in, hoping to comprehend at least some of it.

Hannah raised her hand, and the circle grew silent.

"The tales that have been passed on to us," she told Killian. "They say that one daughter is born to Ama's line who can change the cycle of life and death."

"She is identified by the mark," Elena added.

"The pentagram," Lottie explained. "Spirit. Earth. Air. Fire. Water."

"The number five is mythical. Magical."

"Five senses."

"Five fingers and toes in each limb."

"Christ had five wounds."

Many women were again speaking at the same time. Killian looked from one to the next. A wave of excitement rolled over those gathered in the room. Many were eager to share.

"Muslims have five pillars of their faith. Five times of prayer each day."

"The medieval knights lived by five virtues. They painted pentagrams on their shields."

"People put them on their houses to protect themselves against evil."

"And against death," Hannah concluded.

Silence fell over the room. Everyone was watching Killian.

"This is crazy," she murmured.

"Is it?" Elena asked gently. "Before you came to the island, did you always talk to dead people?"

Killian took a sharp breath.

Hannah took a step toward her. "Sweetheart, you are Ama."

"What does that mean?"

"The legend tells us that there exists a connection between the Aquarians and Ama's descendents," Elena answered. "The story says that one day the sea king's son will choose Ama over going back to his people. When that happens, everyone on this island will become immortal."

Killian stared at the innkeeper, trying to grasp what was just said.

"But what of his people? His destiny?" she asked.

"We become his people. He chooses you. He saves your life."

"You saw the enclosure in the cemetery," Hannah added. "Your mother. Your grandmother. All those women died young."

"That's part of your destiny, too, if you leave here," Elena explained. "Leave Cuttylea Island and you will have a daughter--"

"And die young," Hannah finished.

Killian hugged her arms to her chest. "Everyone dies. I'm not afraid."

"Not now. You have nothing to protect. No child to worry about," her aunt told her. "I was in that hospital room with your mother before she died. I saw the pain she had to endure. She shared her grief with me that she would not be there for you. Not watch you grow up. Not be part of your life."

Tears stung Killian's eyes. She couldn't stop them.

"She asked me to bring you here. To offer you this chance. She wanted you to have what she turned her back on."

"You can make a difference," Elena added.

"For your own life."

"For ours."

"Perth will stay if you ask him to."

"You have the power to keep him here."

Once again, they were all talking at the same time. She forced herself not to listen. She didn't want to hear their troubles.

As for herself, Killian didn't care if she died young. Her mother was dead. She couldn't bring her back.

She thought of Perth. Of how she would never use him. She'd never hold him back from his destiny to save herself. Or to save these people.

She couldn't do that to him. She looked around her at the animated faces. Walt was still staring down at his hands. She turned finally to Hannah.

"No. I won't do it. I'm sorry. I can't help you."

Pushing through the circle of stunned islanders, she ran out of the Tower and into the storm.

CHAPTER 26

She needed to get off this island.

Killian had been up all night thinking about it. There had been plenty of tears. So many questions. Every answer just led to more confusion. Perth was at the center of it all. How she felt about him. How she would never hurt or betray him, no matter what the reward. The bottom line was that she had to leave Cuttylea. Her mother had done the same thing. And so had the women of her family before her.

After she left the Tower, no one came after her. And there had been no sign of Lynx, either. Before she got home, the wind-driven sheets of rain had begun. This morning, the storm was still raging.

When Killian went down to the kitchen, Hannah made no mention of what had been said to her last night. On the way to work, she passed a few familiar faces. A smile, a friendly nod, a cheerful 'Good morning' through the rain was the extent of it. Killian knew she was in no physical danger. At least not from the villagers. They needed her.

Lynx was a different story.

Elena was busy in the kitchen when Killian arrived at the inn. She had seen Ruth and Lottie in the large downstairs window, holding hands and staring out at the harbor as the rain pelted the glass. They weren't looking at her, and she'd picked up bits of their quiet conversation. They were discussing the kind of flowers they wanted planted on their graves.

Not *everyone* would die when Perth left. Killian had figured that much. But there were many who had been living on borrowed time for the last twenty years or so. People like Ruth, Lottie, Hannah, and most likely Walt because of his illness. They'd all die.

The tight knot suddenly forming in her throat was wrong. So why was she feeling it?

Killian picked up the phone at the registration desk. Her calls to her father went to voicemail for both home and cell numbers. He could have been in dozen places on a Saturday morning at the end of June. She didn't leave a message. She didn't know what to say, except that she wanted to go back to Connecticut.

She dialed his cell phone again. This time she decided to leave a message.

"Hi, Dad. It's Killian. I've had a little change of plan. I don't want to stay on Cuttylea for the summer." Her voice was trembling. She paused and took a couple of quick breaths, keeping her emotions under control. "I'll probably take the midweek ferry back to Hyannis and catch a bus from there to either Southbury or Waterbury. I'll call you again in a couple of days to give you a better idea of my plans. I hope that's okay. Thanks. Love you."

She ended the call and stabbed at the tears that were rolling down her cheeks. Like it or not, her father was the only one she had left in this world. Solid in his own way, she knew what he was and what her life with his family would be like. No surprises. No life and death decisions.

The inn was booked to capacity. Even so, Killian was the only help Elena had that early in the morning. Pulling herself together, she walked into the kitchen. The breakfast trays for the cottages were ready to go.

"There's a poncho on the hook on the wall by the back door," Elena told her. "Be careful walking down the path. It gets slippery when it's raining like this."

Killian pulled on the raingear and came back for the trays.

"I already left a message for my father," she told Elena. "I'll be leaving the island sometime during the week."

The innkeeper's face was grim. The gray eyes were sad, but she nodded in understanding. "I'm sorry to see you go. But you have to do what's right for you."

"Did it happen the same way with my mother?" Killian blurted out. "Finding the truth and then leaving?"

Elena took her time spreading icing on pastries she'd just taken out of the oven.

"It wasn't exactly the same," she replied finally, meeting Killian's gaze. "Ama came here several summers before the deciding year. And Hannah was her only true family."

Killian remembered how fondly her mother talked of those summers. They were some of the best days of her youth.

"The blue hole didn't open until the very end of that last summer. And Ama...well, there wasn't the same chemistry between her and the Aquarian. Nothing like the bond between you and Perth."

Killian didn't deny it. She knew her relationship with Perth was different from anything she'd ever imagined possible with a boy her age. Still, she thought they had been very discreet. She wondered what it was about them that everyone noticed.

"At the end of that summer, the blue hole opened, and we finally told Ama. We thought she might still have a chance to convince him to stay. But she wanted no part in it. I know it hurt her, but she left the island." Elena shrugged. "That was it. They both left. That's the last time I saw either of them."

"And then people died."

The innkeeper nodded. "It was their time."

Killian stared at the weathered skin of the woman's hand. Blue veins disappeared under the cuff of her shirt. "How old are you, if you don't mind me asking?"

Elena turned to her in surprise. She smiled. "Seventy-nine."

It was senseless to say that she didn't look or act anything like her age. "You'll live through this. Won't you?"

She gave a noncommittal shrug. "I suppose I'll be at the mercy of my age. I haven't seen a doctor in over twenty years. Cancer, heart disease, stroke. Something might pop up. But death doesn't scare me."

"Then why do you worry about the legend and immortality and the rest of it?"

"Because it's a way of life for us. It's a kind of ritual torch passed on from generations ago. We do as our mothers did before us. You don't break with tradition without reason, do you? It's difficult to explain."

And it was difficult to understand, Killian thought. She was born with a pentagram on her back. But she wouldn't allow a birthmark dictate her actions, plan her future. In her mind, tradition only went so far. A person had to be free to choose. *She* had to be free to choose.

At the same time, she wondered if, years from now, she'd become her mother. And if she'd want her daughter to be faced with this decision, too.

Only time would tell.

She picked up the breakfast tray. A moment later, she was fighting the wind-driven rain.

Killian looked down toward the harbor, wondering where Perth could be. The steel-colored sky blended in with the stormy white-capped sea. The boats by the dock danced and rolled before the gusting wind. Killian held on tight to the tray and picked her way along the slippery gravel path. As she came to the corner of the cottage at the bottom of the hill, she heard Davenport's raised voice. She hesitated. The man was clearly annoyed.

"Check the spelling again. J-O-N-S-O-N. Got that?"

She'd seen Davenport and the other researchers using satellite phones. The benefits of being employed by the state.

"Yes, Boston! And the surrounding counties. It would have been issued twenty years ago. Come on, there has to be a birth certificate."

Anger raised the hackles on Killian's neck. He was checking on Perth.

"How about the social security number?"

A chill ran down Killian's spine. She remembered the blood test.

"Check with the university. They have it on file. Yes, hack into their system, if you have to. And don't forget the death notices for the island population. Twenty years. Yeah! There's definitely something strange going on here. Send all of it to me."

She continued around the corner of the cottage. She could see Davenport pacing back and forth on the porch. He continued to list the things he wanted the person on the line to pull together. She had a feeling every oddity about the islanders could somehow be explained. Still, Killian's mind grew feverish with worry at what the results of the blood test could do to Perth.

"I want the blood test results the same day they come back. Send the .pdf file to my phone." Davenport stopped, noticing Killian. "That's it for now. I don't know if we'll get out on the boat today or not. Call me later."

He pocketed the phone and motioned to her to approach. "Good. You're here. Breakfast. Come up and get out of the rain."

Killian's entire body shook. Worry about what she'd done by bringing Perth to this man was ripping at her insides. She wanted to lash out at him, but she had to check her temper. That wouldn't help anything.

She hurried up on the porch and put the tray on the table. She wasn't about to set the food out for him. He could do that for himself.

"So where's your friend today?"

"Couldn't tell you," she tossed over her shoulder as she ran down the steps. A moment later, she was climbing the gravel path toward the inn.

Killian shook off the poncho and hung it on the hook. Elena was in the kitchen, putting the finishing touches on some breakfast dishes.

Amanda had apparently just come in to work. She was heading out toward the dining room with two glasses of orange juice in her hands. She stopped when she saw Killian.

"My God, what happened last night? Is Perth okay? Where did you go?"

"Not now," Killian told her.

"Amanda, hurry back for these orders," Elena called from the grill.

"Okay."

Killian went directly to the innkeeper. "I need to talk to you…right now."

Elena glanced at her as she slid two plates of food onto the serving station.

"It's *really* important." Killian walked toward the pantry.

"What's wrong?" the innkeeper asked in a low voice, following her in and closing the door.

"A couple of days ago. No, it was…" Killian closed her eyes, trying to concentrate. "Wednesday. It was Wednesday. Davenport took Perth's blood."

Elena's face immediately went pale. "Why?"

"Davenport was Walt's doctor. Years back, in Boston. He told me about Walt's blood disorder. He was sure it had been passed on, father to son. So I told Perth, and he decided to have the scientist test him for it."

"Oh, no." Elena leaned heavily against a cabinet.

"Why 'oh, no'? What does that mean? What's the result is going be? Is Perth going to be in trouble?"

"He breathes under the water, sweetheart," the older woman quietly drawled the words. "I'm no genius, but I doubt if his blood chemistry looks anything like yours and mine."

Killian had decided to leave the island so she wouldn't interfere in his future. It was too late. She'd gotten him into worse trouble. All of them.

"I've read enough about people like Davenport. If he suspects Perth is any different than the rest of us, he'll dissect him like a fetal pig on his kitchen table," Elena warned. "Did he tell you anything this morning?"

"No. He's waiting for the results of the blood test. But he's also snooping around, trying to find a birth certificate and social security number for him. And that's not the end of it. I heard him ask someone on the phone about checking death records on the island."

"He can waste all the time he wants on that," she said. "The most important thing is that we have to warn Perth. We have to keep him away from Davenport."

Killian remembered the mention of the blue hole last night. It was happening, but she had no clue if it would be hours or days before he was gone.

"You have to go and find Perth. Warn him."

"What do I tell him? He doesn't know any of these things, does he? About who he really is, I mean."

"No." Elena put her hand on Killian's shoulder. Strong fingers gripped bone and flesh. She looked into her eyes. "For now, at least, you're one of us. The most important part of our job on this island, the very core of our existence, is to protect Perth. That's why the Aquarians left him with us. Do you know what I'm asking you to do?"

"Keep him away from Davenport until it's time for him to...to go."

Elena nodded.

The rain continued to sweep down in wild gusts on the village. Locals and people whose boats were in the harbor, waiting out the storm, hurried from shop to shop, their brightly colored raingear pulled tight against the storm.

Killian ran all the way up the hill from the inn to Hannah's cottage. She hadn't seen Perth since he disappeared after the fight at the party. She guessed he must be working his oyster beds at the salt pond. Still, she wanted to check with Walt first to make sure.

Hannah wasn't home, but the keys to the cart were on the kitchen counter. Next door, no one answered her knock. Killian moved around to the ramp door coming out of the kitchen and knocked there. Again, no answer.

Perth's father rarely left the house. She knocked again, louder.

"Walt. It's Killian. I hope it's okay; I'm coming in." She turned the knob and pushed the door open.

The kitchen was dark. The lights to the rest of the house were off, too. Killian stepped in and closed the door behind her.

"Walt?" she called out.

The rain was drumming on the roof and windows. The wind was whistling in the chimney. But there were other sounds, too.

The dull hollow ring of a glass thudding on a wooden surface. A page turning. She followed the sounds to the sitting room at the back of the house. Walt in his wheelchair. Books and newspapers and albums littered the floor, spilling off a table. The bottom shelf of the bookcase was in total disarray.

He seemed lost in his own world.

"Walt?" she called softly.

He never raised his head from the photo album he had open on his lap. An empty glass lay on its side on an end table beside him. A nearly empty bottle of Scotch sat beside it. He was stooped over the pictures.

"Did I ever show you pictures of my wife?"

Killian took a step into the room. She noticed the tears on his face.

"No, you never did."

"My wife Paula." He shook his head. "I was the sick one. She wasn't supposed to go before me."

Killian remembered hearing how Walt's wife died in the same car accident that put him in the wheelchair.

He tapped a finger on a page, tilted the album, motioning to her to look at the photograph. Killian pulled up a chair and sat next to him. She could tell that he'd been drinking for a while.

"She was three months pregnant in this picture."

Now that Killian knew the truth, she didn't look for any resemblance between Perth and Walt's wife. In the photograph, the young woman's face radiated happiness. A much younger Walt had his arm wrapped around her. They were on a boat with a golden sunset lighting up Boston's skyline in the background.

"She lost the baby just a few days later," Walt said.

He picked up the bottle, righted the glass, and refilled it. He took a drink.

"Later on, we found out that it was for the best. Any child of mine would have been affected by my disease." He touched the smiling face of his dead wife. "But I was supposed to go first."

Walt had no idea that Davenport was waiting right now for the results of Perth's blood test. Killian decided there was no reason for him to know. At least, not at the moment. Not when he was like this.

"I need to find Perth. Do you know where he is?" she asked gently. "Is he at the salt pond?"

The gaze never lifted off the open page of the album. He was again lost in his own sad world. She was about to go when he roused himself angrily.

"That bastard Davenport was always so happy to remind us that we were living on borrowed time. Time *he* was giving us. Like he was God!"

"Why did you keep going to him?"

"Paula wanted me to," he growled. "He was the only one in the country doing research on this damn blood disorder. She didn't want me to give up. But I hated his attitude."

"Was his research doing any good?"

"Hell, no," Walt snapped. "We were all dying. One by one, we were dying. And I know for a fact that he was fudging the results. It all came out later. Any positive result was blown out of proportion. And so many of the deaths were reported under 'other causes'. That bastard didn't believe in rules and honesty. Doesn't believe in it. All he's ever wanted was fame. Headlines!"

"But you lived."

"Not because of him."

He turned a few pages of the album. The pictures now showed Cuttylea Island. A blond-haired toddler running down a grassy hill toward the beach.

"Hannah came and visited me in Boston soon after the accident. I don't know how she found me. I heard later that they'd voted and picked me. She seemed nice, honest, and genuinely caring. She gave me this long song-and-dance about adoption papers that Paula started for a baby in foster care out on Cuttylea Island."

Killian couldn't imagine why the islanders had chosen a paraplegic widower.

"I knew of no such plans. I knew that Paula would never have done that without telling me. Still, I came out here to see the baby. Of course, they told me right away that the entire story about the adoption papers was bullshit."

"But you stayed."

"How could I not? Paula always wanted a child, but we couldn't have one. And then I saw Perth, this healthy baby who would grow up and thrive, carrying nothing of my curse." He sighed deeply, staring at the sea-green eyes smiling into the camera.

"And you knew your illness would go away, too, so long as you were on the island." Killian was surprised by her own sharp tone.

"I never believed it, at first." The misty eyes turned to her. "The same way, deep down, you don't believe any of the stuff they were telling you last night. It all comes across as nonsense. It did to me. There are days that it still does."

Killian hadn't totally decided what to believe or not to believe.

"I was grieving for my wife. So I decided to take it one day at a time."

"And here you are, twenty years later," she said much more gently.

Walt's gaze returned to the photo album. He turned a page. "Yes, here we are, twenty years later, and I'm about to lose someone I love as much as I loved Paula. I love Perth more than if he was my own flesh and blood."

"Don't you want him to go back to...to where he belongs?"

"I do. I do," he said in protest. "I want him to have what's his. And at the same time, I *want* to go to where Paula's been waiting for me. Unlike the rest of them, I'm ready to die. I want to."

Her hand reached for Walt's. Their fingers entwined. Tears burned in her eyes as she felt Walt's emotions spill over.

Killian wanted to think these people were scheming and malicious. But they weren't. They did what they thought was right. They acted as they thought they should. And they hurt no one. Not yet, anyway.

"It's important for me to find Perth," she said again. "Do you know if he's at the salt pond?"

Walt lifted his head, trying to focus on her. "I haven't seen Perth since yesterday. I don't know where he is. But I'll tell you one thing. It's not like him to stay away this long. Not without coming home and checking on me."

CHAPTER 27

"It's been two days, Hannah. Is he gone? Is that why he hasn't come home?"

Killian never went back to work on Saturday. This morning, either. For the past two days, she'd spent every free minute of her day looking for Perth.

Back and forth to the salt pond. Back to Walt's cottage. Out to Squibnocket Point. Back to the cottage. Nothing.

She couldn't find him. No one had seen him. It hurt her to think that she hadn't had a chance to say goodbye. But more important, she was terrified that something was seriously wrong.

Davenport was still at the inn. That should have been a relief. But it wasn't. What if he'd already done something to Perth? Visions of his people capturing him and taking him away kept gnawing at her. Each time, she had to make sure the research vessel was still in the harbor.

"I've been through this before, don't forget," Hannah told her. She'd just returned to the cottage after the Sunday service. "The storm comes when the blue hole begins to open. It takes a while. Then, when Aquarian returns to his people, the storm immediately lets up."

It was raining even harder today, and the winds were still howling. The road running up from the harbor was already chewed up from streams of rushing water.

"Maybe this is a hurricane," Killian suggested. "Or just some coastal storm having nothing to do with Aquarians or a blue hole."

Hannah immediately shook her head. "I've never known Lynx to be wrong. Besides, Thomas has been watching it on the radar. The storm is centered around and over Cuttylea. The mainland coasts are mostly clear. The same is true for the Elizabeth Islands running to our west. No, this is definitely the blue hole. The Aquarians are getting ready to take back what's theirs."

Killian paced the kitchen floor. She wondered if it would make sense to go to the salt pond again.

"The ferry from Hyannis won't run until the storm lifts. The Coast Guard has a small-boat advisory out for all recreational boats to stay clear, too. It would be suicide for anyone to go out in this."

Killian knew what Hannah was saying. She couldn't leave the island. Not yet. Everything that was happening now no longer had anything to do with her. Perth was the concern. And after what she'd heard Walt say about Davenport, there was more reason to fear how far the scientist would go if anything unusual happened to pop up on his radar.

"What if the research people get wind of what's going on?"

"Elena is keeping a close eye on the cottages," Hannah said.

Killian rubbed her neck. When she thought about Davenport, her head began to ache. Still, he couldn't just abduct someone and make them vanish into thin air.

"How's Elena doing at the inn, anyway? I haven't been any help to her."

"She's managing. She hired some of the friends of the other girls to help temporarily. They're stuck here for the weekend, anyway." She touched Killian's arm gently. "You don't have to worry about her. You have more important things to do."

Like finding Perth and warning him. She hadn't done too well with that so far.

"Can I take your cart again?"

"Absolutely. Where are you going?"

"I don't know. Back to the salt pond. Check the beaches. Maybe Squibnocket Point. It doesn't do much good for me to stay here."

Every time Killian had gone back and forth to the salt pond these past few days, she'd been keeping her eye peeled for Lynx. Though she feared him, she actually hoped she would run into him. She wanted to tell him that she was no threat. That she would not stand in the way of Perth going back to his people. But she was also worried about Perth. Of anyone on the island, she figured Lynx had the best chance of knowing where he was.

They could call it whatever they wanted. These wind gusts and cold rain whipping almost sideways sure felt like a hurricane.

Killian snapped up the canvas sides of the cart and started in the direction of the salt pond first. It wasn't long before she realized she had to change her plans. Downed trees had totally blocked the road.

She turned around and drove back toward the village. Coming over the hill, she saw the inn's bright yellow cart disappearing down the lane toward Hannah's and Walt's cottages.

She stopped at the end of the lane. The cart pulled up in front of Walt's place. Even through the blinding rain, she saw it was Davenport climbing out and running inside.

CHAPTER 28

Killian parked her cart next to Davenport's. The screen door by the ramp was banging against the frame intermittently with the howling wind.

Jumping out, she ran to the door and stood still. The overhang offered little protection from the rain, but she could hear the conversation inside.

"I don't care what those results said. You will leave my son alone."

"Your son? A fake birth certificate and social security card doesn't make him your son. Your actions give you a one-way ticket to jail, Walt. He's not yours. Your wife never delivered any child. There's no birth record for any Perth Jonson. Whoever he is...whatever he is...the state does not look kindly on child kidnapping."

"You have no right to barge in my house like this. Get out." Walt's shouts were louder than the storm raging overhead.

"Only after you tell me where the hell you're hiding him."

"And why would I do that?"

"Because you owe me."

"Owe you what?"

"Your life. You're alive because of me. You owe me credit for all I've done."

"You're one crazy bastard. You think because of some half-assed research experiments—crap that you couldn't get to work—I should hand over my kid to you. And why, so you can continue your research?"

"Okay. Let me explain it to you loud and clear. You hand Perth over to me. I'll resume the studies. If not, I tell the world the truth about him."

"What truth?"

"That he's not human."

Killian stepped away from the door and ran to her cart. She had to find Perth. She had to warn him. The storm ravaging the island was a gift; she had a chance to find Perth before Davenport did.

She headed down toward the harbor. The gusts rocked the cart, threatening to tip it over. The canvas doors couldn't hold back the rain from coming through. Hannah had given her a dry blanket, and she pushed it behind her. The temperature had dropped substantially since the storm started. Whatever Perth's abilities were, spending so many hours in the storm-tossed ocean—if that's where he was—had to be taking a toll on him.

The road running down to the water was empty. In the harbor, the boats were buttoned up tight.

Killian's eyes were drawn to the line of summer houses overlooking the harbor. She saw several people on the porch of one. They were trying to nail a sheet of plywood over a large window. From this distance, she guessed the property was not far from the house Brittany and Liz and Amanda were renting.

She hadn't seen Eric since the night of the party. She'd seen Brittany and Liz only in passing. Neither had brought it up. Killian figured Eric wouldn't dare make any complaint, considering he got exactly what he deserved.

The particulars of that night came back to her. Killian's head began to ache again, and she felt a sense of helplessness and fear.

And then Perth was there in her head.

She remembered what he told her.

You're the one. The one in my head. I can't shake you.

And that night wasn't the only time he'd come to her rescue. She had needed him the day she'd fallen off the cliff by the Tower into the salt pond. He was there, helping her, bringing her back to life.

Killian's fingers gripped the steering wheel of the cart and turned it sharply to the right. She had an idea. It was insane, but she knew she had to do it.

No one else was foolish enough to be on the beach in this weather. A month ago, she would have been too terrified to come out in this. Killian drove the cart until the lane became deep sand. Farther down the beach, she could make out the roof of an open picnic pavilion.

The cart struggled along, but Killian was able to reach the building. She grabbed the blanket and stepped into the covered structure.

The wooden pavilion had a roof but no walls. Stinging sand whipped through on the gusting wind. A couple of picnic tables away from the water were somewhat dry.

The Squibnocket reefs were just barely visible to her right. Killian watched waves crash with tremendous violence onto the beach. Like foraging soldiers, the waves pillaged the land, dragging back spoils from the beach—shells and sand and rock.

There was no one in sight.

"Perth!" she shouted into the wind.

She had to do it. If he was out there in the ocean, he'd come for her. And if he wasn't...well, Killian still had to try before Davenport found him.

Having made up her mind, she peeled off the windbreaker. She kicked off her shoes and tucked them with the blanket on one of the drier picnic tables.

Sheets of rain and sand stung her when she stepped out of the pavilion. The roar of the ocean grew even more menacing as she crossed the beach. Her tee-shirt and shorts were sticking to her body before she reached the water's edge. She shivered with cold and fear of the monster lying dead ahead of her.

"I need you, Perth!" she shouted as loud as she could. The wind threw the words back in her face.

A large wave boomed and crashed, racing up the beach and swirling around her legs. Retreating water gouged the sand, dragging away her footing.

"I'm not giving up!"

Killian followed the receding wave and stepped into the ocean. The water was warm compared to the biting wind.

"Come for me, Perth! I know you'll save me."

Knee deep in the water, Killian took one step and was suddenly chest deep as the next wave curled and crashed over her. She struggled to keep her footing, but the powerful undertow dragged her away from the beach much faster than she'd intended.

And then the bottom fell away. Killian's nose and mouth immediately filled with the brine. Just as she was able to get her head above the stormy ocean surface, another wave crashed viciously over her. Like a rag doll, she was wrapped in the arms of the angry current and pulled under, only to be rolled and pummeled along the sandy bottom.

She struggled and pushed to the surface once more. Another wave. Another moment of chaos in which she had no idea which way was up. Her strength was failing her. She couldn't fight much longer.

Her eyes opened wide. She saw only swirling currents, funnels of sand and seaweed fragments. She stopped struggling and relaxed her arms and legs and felt herself float downward.

An angry storm raged at the surface, but a peaceful stillness waited for her below. A familiar sensation coursed through her body. Similar to what she'd sensed at the salt pond when she'd fallen from the cliff. She had no fear. No worries. She felt safe down here.

This was where she belonged. Voices were calling to her. Whispers encouraging her to join them.

She thought of the reefs off Squibnocket Point. She thought of the many people who'd drowned along this shoreline. She recalled the pleading words of that mother, urging Killian to save her children. She could hear the dead.

She was floating in a vast watery grave. But she'd be safe. She could stay here.

Then, like a shark, he cut through the water, searching her out. She saw him approach. Perth was swimming toward her at an incredible speed.

Suddenly, Killian found herself trying to get away. She didn't want to be saved. She was home.

There was no escaping him. Perth grabbed her by the waist, and the two of them rocketed toward the surface. She fought him, but he was stronger, faster.

When they broke through, the struggle to take air into her lungs was another shock to her system. Coughing and crying, she twisted in his arms, but he held her as if she were a part of him. He started swimming toward the now distant beach.

Once again, with the familiar taste of air, came the fear of drowning. She saw he was trying to save her. She stopped fighting him.

Waves foamed around them, and the current tried to pull them out to sea. Perth's strength didn't seem to match the tide. She was too much of a dead weight. He fought harder, and she kicked with her legs.

It was as if an eon passed before she felt the sandy bottom. Perth's face was white, and he was almost too weak to stand up. Another foaming wave battered at them. Killian took over what he'd been doing a moment ago. With her arms around his waist, she held him up as well as she could, pulling him toward the beach.

It was a miracle when they staggered past the crashing surf. Perth was struggling to catch his breath. She held on tight, supporting his weight.

"Come on. Please. We're almost there."

The picnic pavilion was now only a few steps away. A blast of wind nearly toppled them into the sand.

"I can't," he gasped. "There's something wrong with me. The air."

For a split second, Killian didn't know if she should push him back into the ocean or just hold him here. He was shaking. The spell had not begun the moment he stepped out of the water, she realized. He'd been struggling the entire time that he was dragging her toward the shore.

"Perth." She lifted his head, looking into his beautiful eyes. Her heart twisted, seeing the confusion in him. He clearly didn't know what was wrong or why he was suffering like this.

Ancient tales. Folklore. Myths she didn't want to believe in. But she'd heard them. The islanders believed them.

Perth needed her. She needed to be part of his life if he was going to survive on land.

Killian kissed him. She touched her lips to his and wrapped her arms around him. He drew back for an instant, as if shocked. Then his mouth immediately sought hers. He sensed the need, too. With the wind swirling around them, his arms brought her body against his, and their passion soared.

Thunder exploded somewhere nearby. Breaking off the kiss, Killian took his hand and pulled him under the shelter of the building.

Perth was still trembling, but his breathing seemed to be getting back to normal. His skin was ice cold. His eyes watched her with something akin to wonder as she sat down on a picnic table. Grabbing the blanket, she draped it over his shoulders.

"What were you doing in that water?" He took her hand. "You could have died."

"You've been missing for so long. No one knew where you were. I was worried about you."

"I was lost. I've never had something like this happen before. I couldn't find my way home. Something was pulling me." He nodded his head toward the water. "And then you were there, in my head. You needed me. I heard your voice, calling to me."

Killian moved into his arms as he wrapped the blanket around her, too. His skin was getting warm. The tee-shirt she was wearing was wet and cold.

His fingers took hold of the bottom hem of her shirt, and she didn't object when he peeled it up over her head. She shivered and helped him pull off her tank top, as well.

Every nerve in her body came alive when he drew her bare skin against his warm chest.

"I need you, Killian. Right now. I never wanted anything in my life more than you." There was urgency in his voice. He spoke like someone starved for air or dying of thirst. His lips closed over hers again.

She tried to hold on to some shred of sanity, but with each passing second the task became more impossible. His hands roamed all over her body, touching her, caressing her. Her body was telling her that she wanted this as much as he did.

His fingers moved down her back to the waistline of her shorts. He was touching the birthmark on her back. Immediately, her skin burned, and Killian gasped. A second later, the heat from his touch was radiating through her, electrifying her. She leaned into him, welcoming everything he was doing to her.

The moment his fingers began to undo the button of her shorts, a point of clarity cut through her desire. She caught his wrist.

"Wait," she told him. "If we do this now, you will never find a way to leave the island."

Both of them were breathless, their faces only inches away. Through the haze of passion, she saw confusion take shape.

"What are you talking about?"

"This thing between us is different from what other people have. You and I will have no say in what happens...afterwards."

She held onto him, trying to talk fast. Trying to tell him everything she knew.

"The painting in the cave; it was an ancient warning. The two people on the wall—the ones in the hut—they were us. You and me. You knew that. That's why you took me there."

It took only a moment for her to tell him the rest. About Lynx showing up at Hannah's door and what she'd learned later about the pentagram on her body and most importantly, what she'd learned about him. She didn't dwell on the fact that the islanders wanted to keep Perth on the island so they could have immortality. There was no need. Killian would have a say in that, and whatever was decided, their desires would not play a part in Perth's fate.

And she felt it was important for him to know that these people cared for him. They had worked hard to keep him safe.

"Aquarians?" he asked, his gaze drawn to the stormy ocean. "I grew up knowing I was different. I just never knew how different."

Killian realized at that moment that her confusion about life was nothing compared to Perth's. She, at least, had a father. And like it or not, she had a home she was familiar with to go back to. Everything lying in Perth's future was completely unknown.

"I need some answers," he said, straightening up.

She pulled on her windbreaker, zipping it up to her chin.

Perth looked very weak.

"I have Hannah's cart here. I'll drive you up to the cottage."

He nodded.

Killian hoped Davenport was gone. She snatched up her wet clothes off the table.

"You shouldn't blame Walt," she said. "Emotionally, he's not doing too well."

"I could never think badly of him. Deep down, I guess I've known for a long time I wasn't his biological son. But he's been the best father anyone could ever ask for."

Killian hadn't realized the extent of his weakness until he started walking beside her to the cart. She put an arm around him.

"What's happening to you?"

"So long in the water, I think I've forgotten how to walk."

The fury of the storm was not easing up, at all. She pulled the blanket higher on his shoulders after he sat in the passenger seat. She raced around the cart and got behind the wheel.

She looked at him as she turned the cart in the sand. "How did you know that Walt wasn't your father?"

"There was nothing there to tell me that he was. Once I was old enough to check the dates, like when he came to the island, nothing matched up. More than that, though, he always avoided any contact with our family on the mainland. I made some inquiries of my own. The parents of Walt's wife Paula are still alive. She has a sister, too. That never made sense. But it didn't matter. In other ways, Walt was everything I wanted him to be."

"Then why did you agree to let Davenport do the blood test?"

"I don't know. I guess I was just hoping that maybe I'd always been wrong. In a way, hoping that I'd have that disease."

"But Walt is really sick. He could die."

"He won't. I won't let him."

The confidence in his healing abilities was no surprise. Killian realized she had yet to tell Perth that people on the island would die when he returned to his people.

The cart bumped up onto the lane. She decided that she wouldn't tell him yet. He didn't need more complications in his life. In the decision he had to make.

"Davenport has your results back. I heard him telling Walt. He knows you're different."

"I'll deal with him later."

The tide was coming in faster and higher than normal. Waves were leaving behind lakes of seawater that were encroaching on the path to the beach. A wrenching sound behind them made her look back in time to see two large patches of shingles being ripped off the roof of the pavilion. Killian and Perth watched them sail off into the sea grass.

"Thank you," he said, reaching over and caressing the back of her hand. "Thank you for coming after me."

Her heart was drumming in her ears. Her emotions were a tight fist lodged in her throat. She couldn't speak the words, but she realized at that moment that she loved him in a way that she'd never loved another person. Passion and friendship. A sense of being complete and absolutely happy when she was with him.

But the impossibility of their situation was a heartbreak she'd already come to terms with.

She forced her face away so he wouldn't see the tears springing to her eyes.

The cart struggled over debris that had blown onto what was left of the road. She maneuvered around huge pools of water and eventually reached slightly higher ground.

"I think Lynx is the person you should see," Killian told him, once she had a handle on her emotions. "He's the one who brought the news of the blue hole, of this door to that other world."

"The keeper of secrets," he murmured, repeating what she'd told him before. "How ironic, considering he can't see or talk."

"He can. But only to certain people."

"You hear him."

"So does Hannah. I heard them. I know they can communicate."

CHAPTER 29

"What's that?"

Perth was staring ahead through the Plexiglas windshield of the cart.

Killian peered through the downpour. A cart was parked across the lane, blocking them. Any of the islanders could have been out searching for Perth.

Her fists tightened on the wheel when she saw two people climb out of the cart. Two researchers who were working for Davenport.

As she slowed, one of them ran up through the rain and pulled open the door on Perth's side.

"Man, am I glad we found you," he said over the wind. "Dr. Davenport has the results of your blood test."

"That right?" Perth asked, his face a mask.

"Yeah. Hate to be the one to tell you, but the bad news is that you tested positive. The good news is that he's been on the phone with the university hospital in Boston. The lab is ready and waiting for you."

Without waiting, the researcher turned and started back toward his cart.

"He isn't going anywhere," Killian called after him. "Not in this weather."

The taller man stood watching them. "Our research vessel can handle this storm. The plan is to take you back to the mainland today and start the treatments tonight. Doc says you'll be just fine. As good as new. Just like your father."

"I said he isn't leaving," she said coldly, reaching over and taking Perth's hand.

"None of this concerns you," he snapped before turning to Perth. "The boat is ready now. The crew had to go through a lot for this—"

"Everything about this, about me, concerns her," Perth growled. "You gave me the message. Now, get out of the way. We have someplace to be."

Killian looked ahead at their cart. Davenport's assistant was already reporting in on a handheld radio. She wondered how far these people would go to take Perth to Boston, whether they'd go so far as to abduct him.

The tall man pressed Perth. "I want you to know that Dr. Davenport is putting a lot of effort into getting you the help you need."

"I didn't ask for any help. Did I?"

"We were told you did. And our directions are to take you back to the boat right away."

"Your directions? In your freaking dreams," Perth said angrily. "Get out of our way."

Killian let the vehicle roll back slightly and pressed her foot on the gas.

"I can't let you go." Stepping to the side of the cart, he reached in and grabbed Perth's arm.

Big mistake. Regardless of his fatigue, Perth gave the tall man a violent shove that sent him sprawling on the wet grass. His partner stood by their cart, clearly trying to decide whether he wanted to tangle with Perth. Before he could, Killian turned the cart off the path and they bumped and rolled back down toward the beach.

"Crap. Crap. Crap." She spat out the words, looking back over her shoulder. "Davenport thinks he's hit the jackpot with that blood test. He's going to have his entire crew on our tale now. He's probably waiting up at Walt's, right now."

"Let's go to the Tower. I want to find Lynx."

"How? We can't go back through the village."

"Keep going this way. We won't be able to go farther than those boulders at the end of the beach, but we can leave the cart and walk the rest of the way."

Killian looked over at him. She wasn't sure Perth was in any condition to walk across the island. But they seemed to have no option.

Perth wasn't getting any weaker. Before they deserted the golf cart and started off on foot, Killian had forced him to down a couple of water bottles and the power bars she had in her backpack. But he wasn't getting any stronger, either.

Tree branches and debris were strewn everywhere from the raging storm, and falling limbs were a real threat.

They'd been trekking through the woods for almost an hour with no sign of anyone. Killian was surprised that the two researchers hadn't followed them.

"I can't believe we haven't seen the Tower yet," she said. "We've got to be getting close."

"We're getting there." Perth never let go of her hand the entire time. "It's straight ahead."

A moment later, the two of them were standing on the road that led from the village to the town dump and the salt pond.

"Not far now," he told her. She could hear the weary edge in his voice. "This path will lead us up to the cliffs."

The trip across the island had been up and down, but they were climbing steadily now. She was tired; she knew he had to be exhausted.

"Tell me what you know about this blue hole?" he asked her after they'd walked a short while in silence.

"They said it's a door of some kind. When it opens, it's time for you to go back to your people."

"My people," he muttered, frustration evident in his tone. "I don't know anything about that. I thought these were my people. How can I go back to something I've never known?"

"You're in danger here," she said quietly.

Killian clung to his hand, knowing that she would lose him too soon.

"This blue hole. Who says it's open?"

"Lynx told Hannah."

"What happens if I'm not ready to go?" he asked, meeting her gaze.

Emotions were running high in both of them. Neither could trust themselves to voice their feelings. She knew that so much had to be pulling at him. She was the least of it. He had to be worrying about Walt. If the time was now that he must go, he wouldn't even be able to say goodbye to him.

"I don't know what will happen," she finally managed to say. "But we both know that Davenport is after you. He has to. You won't be safe here on the island. Maybe not anywhere."

"You worry about Davenport too much."

"And you don't worry enough," she said, squeezing his hand. "You've been protected here. People like him are cruel and bitter and ruthless. You don't know how much damage they can do."

"What could he possibly gain by taking me back to Boston?"

"Whatever showed up on your blood test has already told him that you don't have the same biological chemistry as other people," she said sadly. "He's seen you. He'll figure it out. In exposing you as an Aquarian, he'll be famous. He'll be on every talk show and on the cover of every magazine in the country."

Cold waves of shame washed through Killian. She was the one responsible for bringing that danger to his door. Perth would have never known or agreed to the test if she hadn't brought it up. She moved closer to him, slipping an arm around his waist as they walked.

"When he has you in Boston, he won't stop at a blood test."

"Davenport is only one man."

"It doesn't matter. He is still connected. And he won't stop. Look at how he's already using the resources of this windmill project."

Perth shrugged, still unconvinced of the danger.

"He'll bring in the media. They'll be swarming all over this island. Nothing will be safe from them," she warned. "Please don't take him so lightly. Don't assume that he can't hurt you. He can. He will."

"I don't care about Davenport. What I'm suffering with knowing that I'll lose you."

He stopped and pulled her into his arms and kissed her.

Instantly, the world around them melted away. All that existed for Killian at that moment was the feel of his lips on hers and the powerful heat of his body. Kissing him back, she wanted to be one with him.

When he pulled back, Killian felt the hard, unkind world come rushing back in like a blast of icy wind from the storm raging around them. With it, she felt deep within her just what she was about to lose.

He turned away, still holding her hand, and led her up the hill. Moments later, the Tower came into view through the line of the trees.

Killian stared at the stark stone structure, looking almost black against the wild, stormy sky. How many children of the Aquarians, she wondered, had passed beneath its walls over the centuries?

"You think Lynx will be inside?" she asked.

"The shack he lives in can't stand up to this weather. It's the most logical place for him to go."

In light of everything, Killian thought 'logical' was such an unreasonable word. As wild as it was before, the storm had intensified dramatically since they left the other side of the island. She held tightly to Perth's arm as they struggled up the hill toward the Tower. The ground was slick with rain, and she had a difficult time finding solid footing. Perth didn't seem to be faring much better.

Killian could see no sign of Lynx.

"Maybe he's not here," she shouted over the roar of the storm.

The noise drowned out her words. Flashes of lightning exploded around them, and Killian could feel the crackle of electricity in the air. Perth ignored it all and pulled her along with him.

Fighting the wind with every step, they finally reached the stone structure. Working their way around the base of the Tower, he led her to the edge of the cliff. Killian stood rooted to the ground, stunned by the sight in front of them.

"What is that?"

Not thirty yards from the face of the cliff, a wall of metal gray water formed a funnel connecting salt pond and sky. The wide, watery tornado foamed, spewing mist and sand, rock and shellfish in every direction. Looking down at the churning surface, Killian saw that Perth's oyster beds at the far end of the salt pond had disappeared. The spinning water spout was working like a drain, pulling everything around it into the depths.

"The blue hole," Killian muttered in disbelief.

The Tower with its pentagram built into the floor was a marker. Beneath the funnel of water lay the passageway to the Aquarian's world. This was where she'd met Lynx the first time, where he'd been standing guard over a sacred site.

Her hand dropped from Perth's arm.

He moved away from her to the very edge of the cliff. He'd dropped the blanket somewhere behind them. His shoulders and arms glistened with rain. The wind blew the hair away from his face. His gaze was focused on the scene below. He looked like a hero from some ancient myth, peering down at the kingdom that held his destiny.

Killian took a step back. Then another. They didn't need Lynx.

This was the place, and now was the time.

"Perth," she whispered, tears mixing with the pouring rain. She had to let him go.

"*PERTH!*" The man's shout came from directly behind them.

Killian turned, shocked to see Davenport striding out onto the rocky ledge. He was staring past them at the funnel. As he went by her, she looked up toward the Tower to see if anyone else was with him. No one.

"Come on," the scientist shouted. "You've got to come back with me."

It took a long moment before Perth even turned to acknowledge the intruder's presence. But Davenport's eyes were now locked on him.

"Let's go. It's essential that we get you to the mainland."

Perth shook his head. "Don't waste your time lying about the blood test results. I'm not going with you."

"I'm telling the truth," Davenport argued. "You come with me to Boston, I'll run some routine tests, get you on the right medication, then we'll get you back here."

A bolt of lightning lit up the air around them, and the immediate crack of thunder shook the earth.

"Why would I do that? Why would I trust you? Why would anyone?"

"You're *not* anyone. You know it and everyone on this island knows it." Davenport shot a quick look at the imposing wall of water. "Listen, I'm giving you a chance to do this on your own before things get ugly."

Killian tried to move out on the cliff toward them, but a gust of wind blasted her. It felt like a huge hand, holding her back. She looked at the scientist again, wondering for the first time if he might be armed. She couldn't see anything beneath the bulky rain gear.

"Don't threaten me. There's nothing you can do to me."

"Think again. I can destroy you. I can wipe out everything you care for on this island."

"Don't listen to him," Killian shouted.

She realized Davenport would use any kind of trickery to get Perth to go along. The creep knew how much Perth cared for his father. And it was obvious that the younger man was physically weak. She thought of the research assistant on the radio down by the beach. Davenport had no doubt already contacted his team. He was trying to keep Perth cornered here until they showed up.

"The blue hole is open, Perth," she continued. "This is it. Go now, while you can."

The scientist shot her a killing glare before turning back to his prize.

"Who are you willing to sacrifice, boy? Walt, who has survived his death sentence by twenty years? That neighbor of yours, Hannah? There is no record at all how old she really is. The others on this island who are over a hundred years old? No one gets sick. No one dies. My friends in the media will have a field day. They'll hit this place like swarm of locusts. They'll take you down first and then destroy everything in their path. The publicity will wipe this precious island of yours off the map. There'll be nothing left that you recognize."

Killian saw Lynx coming out of the woods. With his stick sweeping the ground in front of him, the strange man approached. His sightless eyes seemed to focus on the back of Davenport as he continued to press Perth.

"I'm giving you this one last chance. Come with me now, and I'll leave your friends out of it entirely."

Perth was looking over Davenport's shoulder at the approaching Lynx.

"No," he said, lifting a hand at Lynx. "I can handle this. I'll deal with him."

It was too late. The scientist turned and saw the ragged blind man just as the ancient Aquarian raised his stick.

Davenport flew upward like a leaf and sailed out over the edge of the cliff. His piercing scream could be heard even above the roar of the storm.

Killian's knees suddenly felt like rubber. She opened her mouth, but Perth's voice rang out before she could say the words.

"That's wrong. I can't let him die."

He took two steps and leaped after Davenport.

No mystical power or force of nature could hold her back. Killian ran to the very edge where Perth had jumped. The column of the water emanated power and seemed to have grown in size. The encroaching funnel beneath was churning up the salt pond. She couldn't see Perth or Davenport.

Killian didn't believe Perth was invulnerable. She'd seen him weakened in the past few days.

Suddenly, Lynx was standing at her side.

"You've got to help Perth," she cried. "He's not strong enough."

"He'll find his way," Lynx replied.

"He won't go, not while he thinks he needs to save a life."

"The stranger does not deserve to live." Lynx turned away from the cliff and started toward the Tower.

"No," she called after him. "Whatever Davenport is, whatever he wants, it doesn't matter. Perth will try to save him, even if it kills him."

Lynx paused for only a moment, and then continued to move away.

"You brought him to the people of this island," Killian shouted. "They raised him and nourished him. You can't leave Perth this way!"

The ragged man kept going.

"Do what you want," she cried. "But I'm going after him."

CHAPTER 30

Buffeted by the high winds, Killian hurried as fast as she could along the cliff's edge. After what felt like eternity, she reached the break in the rock face where she and Perth had climbed up the day she'd fallen.

The descent was treacherous, the rocks slippery and the path a muddy river. The days of wind and rain had loosened any grip she managed to get a hold of. But she didn't give up. The mist emanating from the funnel of water blocked her view of everything below.

Her muddy sneakers skidded on a broad slick rock, and she lost her hold of some bushy growth she'd grabbed for support. She cried out as she fell a dozen feet, landing on a protruding ledge. A bolt of lightning struck the cliff face, and the concussion nearly dislodged her again. The air crackled as she tried to catch her breath.

Killian didn't know what she'd be good for once she reached the pond's edge, but she knew that Perth seemed to revive in some way when he was with her.

She kept going. Rock gave way to muddy path, which in turn gave way to loose stone, sending her sliding again.

There was nothing graceful about her next fall. She gasped, the wind knocked from her body as she landed with a painful thud on her back on a flat ledge of stone.

She rolled over and pushed herself to her knees. The roar of the funnel was deafening here. Squinting up at the Tower through the rain and mist, she saw an eerie image at the top of the cliff. Like some mythical wizard watching the spectacle before him, Lynx stood on the ledge, his ragged clothes flying in the wind.

Edging her way off the rock, she continued down.

Finally reaching what was left of the beach at the edge of the salt pond, Killian felt like she had landed in the belly of the whale. She could see nothing of the Tower or anything else.

The thick dark mist and stinging sand swirled in the air. Fish and seaweed were strewn along the water's edge. The funnel had grown even larger, sucking everything to its center. Killian's head ached from the pounding roar.

She stepped into the roiling water of the pond, moving toward the center of the storm.

"*PERTH!*" she cried out.

Immediately, she felt the wet slap of the gusting wind, pushing her back.

"I'm here, Perth! I'm here if you need me."

The roar only became louder. Then, straight ahead, she saw a shape move near the funnel's edge. A voice was calling to her. Killian stepped into deeper water and was immediately pitched to her knees by the wind.

Her face went into the water. The salt water stung her cuts and scrapes, and she tasted brine and sand. She was able to find her footing again. She staggered to her feet. A shadowy figure struggled to swim away from the funnel, dragging a body with him.

"Perth." She moved toward them.

Whatever fear she once had of drowning and storms was gone, and she focused on the man coming toward her.

Killian took a few steps toward him and saw Perth go under. She pushed deeper--waist deep, chest deep--until she could barely keep her head above the water. She couldn't see him, and panic washed through her.

Suddenly, Perth surfaced a few feet from her with Davenport's arm draped across his shoulder. She reached out to him. He took her hand, and they moved closer to the shore.

"Help me with him."

Killian was more worried about Perth. His face was as pale as the unconscious scientist he was carrying. She grabbed Davenport's other arm, and the two of them worked together to haul him to the beach.

Dropping the man on his back on the sand, Perth sank to his knees a few feet away.

"Check on him," he said over the noise of the storm. "See if he's still breathing."

Killian crouched down. His glasses and rain jacket were gone, and his face was a deathly gray. His eyes were open, but they were dull and lifeless. There was no breath, no movement, at all. She pressed her finger against his neck, feeling for a pulse. There was nothing.

"He's dead," she told Perth.

Help me.

The voice jolted Killian. She looked up at the roaring funnel looming above them.

I know you hear me. Please…help me.

Killian's gaze dropped to the body lying on the sand. Her hand shook as she again felt for the man's pulse. Nothing.

He can save me. Please tell him to save me.

"He's speaking to me," she said, unable to tear her gaze from the man's face. His eyes were on her.

He came after me. He tried to save me. It's not too late. I don't want to die.

"He says you can save him," she said.

Placing his palm on the man's chest, Perth focused his attention solely on Davenport. She moved back, giving him the space to do what he needed to do.

She *could* hear the dead—or perhaps just those who had yet to 'cross over'. The face of the young mother on the dock during the storm rushed back into her mind. Perhaps there had been time for Perth to save her life, too. But she had chosen her two boys' lives over her own.

Killian sank to her knees in the sand. She watched Perth as her mind drifted to her own mother. Knowing now the power of life here on the island, she wondered why Hannah hadn't brought Ama back here to heal.

Spending nights and days in the hospital, Killian had seen so many sick, suffering people. Old and young. Children struggling against cancers that afflicted them. She'd seen a parent's anguish at the sight of a child dying before her eyes.

Killian had no clue how this pact with the Aquarians worked or why some fifty people on this island were privileged enough to benefit from it. Where was the justice in that?

Davenport's body suddenly jerked. Coughing up water, he sputtered, gagged, and struggled for breath.

Killian guessed there would be no answers to her questions. She moved to Perth's side.

The scientist took a breath and then another. The spark of life was back in the eyes. He watched the two of them in bewilderment.

The sound of far off shouts from above reached them.

"You have to go," Killian whispered to Perth, pulling at his arm. "He'll live."

He looked at her, unable to hide the sadness.

"Please," she begged him.

He started to rise, but Davenport caught his wrist.

"I...I'm sorry."

Killian was surprised to hear the raw emotion in older man's voice.

"You owe me," Perth said coldly.

"I...I know." Davenport stopped, exhausted from the exertion.

Killian tugged at Perth's elbow. He was weak, but he managed to stand up.

"Lean on me," she said, slipping her head under his arm. Together, they walked to the edge of the water.

"I can't just leave like this. Cuttylea is my home."

"This island *was* your home. People grow. The move on to other places. They pursue different lives."

"I'm not like other people."

Killian held on to him. "No, you're not. But you told me yourself that you've always been searching, looking for something. A door. You knew you had to leave this island. Now, it's time."

"Walt. I have to speak to him. To say goodbye. He needs to know that he will always be my father. I have to explain."

The voices were coming closer. She couldn't chance anyone hurting Perth.

"Walt knows what you have to do," she said hurriedly. "He's known from the beginning that your time here was limited."

"There are others on the island that I need to see, at least one last time."

Killian knew exactly how he felt. Leaving her mother's bedside at the hospital had been the most painful moment of her life. She had known Ama was dead, but it made no difference. She couldn't bring herself to tell Perth that the people of this island had destinies of their own.

"You have to go now. This storm is getting worse by the minute. You saw what Lynx did to protect you. Your people are waiting for you. They want you back."

He stood, his feet planted in the wet sand. His hand cupped her face. His eyes bore into hers. "Killian, I can't leave you."

"You have to," she said, raising herself up and brushing her lips against his. No matter how hard she tried, she couldn't stop the tears from falling.

"There has to be another way."

She shook her head. "You're not safe here. Today, it was Davenport. Tomorrow, it will be someone else. We'll be fine here, but you have to go to your people. It's the only place that you'll be safe."

She was helpless when he gathered her in his arms and kissed her. She felt as if, somewhere on this journey, they had become one, body and soul. She pushed at his chest and stepped back.

"You will always be the one," she whispered.

"Killian, I--"

"Don't say it," she told him sternly, taking another step back. "Go, Perth. Please."

The raw knot of emotions was about to choke her. Every inch of her body struggled to go to him, but she willed herself to stay where she was.

Finally, he turned and went into the water. She watched him swim away through the mist. When he reached the roaring column of water, he dove beneath the surface and disappeared.

Killian looked after him for a long time and then lifted her face to the pelting rain, knowing there would be no end to the tears.

CHAPTER 31

Killian sat beside Davenport, staring at the wall of water that seemed to be growing less intense with every passing minute. The mist continued to swirl around her, and there were voices in her head.

Whether they came from the land or the sea, whether they belonged to the dead or to the living, she didn't care. She had just lost the first man she'd ever loved.

"Why did he save me?" Davenport asked, breaking into her solitude.

"He must have believed there was some goodness left in you. He thought you were worth saving."

Killian closed her eyes. The wind was lessening. The rain stopped. Hannah's prediction was coming true. The Aquarians now had what they'd come after. The storm was about to lift.

As she helped the man up, Killian fought back the burning in her throat. She let him lean on her as they made their way along the beach. She had to help Davenport take each step. He was weak and shaken.

She couldn't look back for fear of falling apart. Perth was gone. The image of him swimming away through the mist would be forever etched in her mind.

Three carts came into view, and Davenport's crew jumped out of the vehicles and surrounded them.

They were all talking at the same time. Davenport took a blanket passed to him by one of his assistants. He leaned heavily against the first cart.

"Is he back on the beach?" someone asked.

"No," Davenport said.

"The island is so small. We can find him."

"No. We're done harassing him. I was wrong," the scientist responded sharply. "I made a mistake. Perth Jonson has his own doctor on the mainland. We're lucky that he's not pressing charges for invading his privacy. All of our careers would be done."

His words silenced them.

"But what about the blood test?" one of them finally ventured.

Davenport pulled the blanket higher on his shoulder. "It was a *mistake*."

Killian stared at the scientist. Perth was right to save him. His brush with death had changed him.

"Let me give you a ride back to the village," Davenport said quietly as the others turned the carts around.

"No," Killian said, shaking her head. "I need to walk."

The older man nodded and then paused before turning away.

'Thank you. Thank you for hearing me. I owe you as much as I owe Perth."

She shrugged. Even the mention of his name felt like a hot shaft being driven into her heart.

"One thing. Who was the lunatic on the cliff? The one with the stick."

She met Davenport's gaze. "You can repay Perth by never mentioning what happened here again…to anyone."

"You can count on it." He placed his hand on her arm. "I'm here to research the potential effect of wind generators on sea life. That's it. I don't know Walt Jonson, and I don't know anything else about anyone living here. How's that?"

Killian nodded. With Perth gone, she wasn't as worried about what Davenport's threats could do to the island. But she knew Perth would want it this way.

Watching them disappear around a bend into the woods, Killian started back. The storm had lifted. The leaves on the trees glistened as the sun broke through, and patches of blue sky began to open up between racing clouds.

As she walked, she could not help thinking of the islanders who might be succumbing right now to age or illness. And if not today, the deathwatch would surely continue in the coming days. She had seen the gravestones of the past.

Covering her face, she let out an angry and frustrated cry. She'd loved and lost, and once again she was losing all those she cared for so much.

This is not the end of it.

Killian's heart stopped. He was back. She looked on in disbelief as Lynx stepped into her path and raised his staff at her.

You shouldn't have meddled.

She was no longer afraid of him, but anger flashed through her.

"I held back the truth," she snapped. "I didn't tell him that everyone he loved would die when he was gone. I made him go. I did what you wanted."

I'm warning you. They will all suffer. You will suffer. This is not over.

Killian's anger turned to confusion as the ragged man turned away.

"He's gone!" she shouted, watching him disappear into the woods. "What more do you want from me?"

CHAPTER 32

"He's gone." Killian's voice shook as she whispered the words to Walt.

Elena and Hannah were already sitting with the grieving man when she came into the cottage. Having seen the storm pass, none of them should have been surprised. Still, her words clearly had a heartbreaking finality for all of them.

Elena sat down on the edge of chair next to him and took Walt's hand. Hannah walked to the window and looked out at the brilliant colors streaking across the late afternoon sky.

"Did he say anything before he went?" Walt asked, his voice thick with emotion.

"He wanted me to tell you goodbye." Killian looked at him through her tears. "He said that you would always be his father."

Walt turned the wheelchair around sharply and faced the bookcases on the wall. Killian saw his shoulders slump despondently.

Elena stared down at her hands. She seemed lost in a world of her own.

"How are Ruth and Lottie?" Killian asked softly.

"They locked themselves in their apartment with the cat. They won't let me in."

Leaning against the wall, Killian hugged her arms tightly around her middle. Death was such a final thing. It was waiting somewhere along the road of life for all of them. Not knowing when and how the end would come was something she'd struggled with since she was a young child. Was it better to have someone you love die instantly in an accident, or to know the end was near and come to terms with it in advance? In her mind, watching them suffer didn't offer any comfort.

Killian glanced again at Hannah. Her back was straight, her head high. Her face showed none of the grief the other two wore so openly.

She knew her great aunt had witnessed this same thing many times before. They'd raised a child in safety and with love. Aquarians had come before and taken what was theirs. Happy lives had been torn apart. People died. A lot of people on this island knew that today would be the end for them. She showed no fear of what most likely lay in store for her this time. It was all just a part of the bargain.

Despite the false pretense in bringing her to the island, Killian loved the old woman. She'd been nothing but kind and caring. Just as she'd been to Ama.

Killian joined her at the window. She put her arm affectionately around the old woman's waist and looked outside at the glowing sky.

Steam was rising from the ground. The patches of soft clouds gave no hint of the storm that had been ravaging the island only hours before. A small seaplane dipped down over the island's breakwater and scudded into the harbor below. Seagulls stretched their wings and floated effortlessly in the soft breeze.

"I'm sorry I disappointed you," Killian said softly.

"Oh, my heavens. I'm not disappointed, my love. Besides, it's not over."

Killian hadn't said a word about running into Lynx. She hadn't told her about the strange man's warning. But before she could ask Hannah about her comment, her aunt smiled and pressed the tips of her fingers against the window.

Killian looked out and saw Perth coming down the lane from the woods.

He never had a chance to get within a dozen yards of the house.

She screamed. She cried. She laughed. She leaped into his arms with such joy that they almost tumbled together onto the muddy lane. But he stood his ground and held her, devouring her mouth in a kiss that matched her eagerness.

"How...? What...? How are you here?" she finally asked, breathless and happy and afraid, but wanting to know.

He put her down. "There was nothing there."

"But the storm. The blue hole. We both saw the funnel. You swam right into it."

"And it drew me in. I had no control, no strength in the spinning current. But at the bottom of it all, there was no door," he told her. "I found my strength coming back while I was in there. I swam to the very center of the thing, but there was nothing there except the bottom of the pond."

"But the storm lifted so suddenly."

"I don't know. If there was ever a hole, maybe it closed."

"Lynx said the door was opening. Why would it close again? I don't understand."

"That makes two of us."

"I saw him on my way back here," she told him. "He said this wasn't over. I don't know what that means, either. What's going to happen now?"

"I have no clue," he told her, taking her hand and kissing her again.

He broke off the kiss abruptly, looking toward the house. She followed his gaze. Walt was outside with Hannah and Elena. They were at the end of the ramp. Perth took her hand and pulled her in their direction.

"The only thing I do know," he whispered in her ear, "is that you and I have each other."

When they reached the cottage, she stood back and basked in the joy of Walt and Perth's reunion. They would have time to find the answers to their questions.

"Killian!" The voice came from the front of Hannah's cottage. The tone, sharp and familiar, plucked a string inside her.

She turned and looked in disbelief. Her father was standing in the lane.

"Dad?" She closed the distance between them in an instant.

There was no reserve in the way he pulled her to his chest.

"My God, what a relief," he murmured. "Are you okay?"

"Of course I'm okay."

"But the phone call? Your message? I was sure you were in trouble. I had to get to you."

Killian couldn't remember exactly what she'd left on his voicemail. "How did you get here with this storm?"

"I chartered a sea plane from New Bedford. I spent the night there, and we took off as soon as the storm let up."

His shirt was wrinkled, his hair standing on end. He hadn't shaved. A wave of affection for him washed through her. He cared enough for her to rush here like this.

Killian looked around her. "You didn't bring Susan and the twins?"

"No. But she wanted me to tell you that your room is ready at home. And that she'll speak to the restaurant manager at the golf club if you want a job when we get back."

Killian stared at him for a moment.

"No, Dad. I'm going to stay. I *want* to stay here," she said quickly to get the words out. She glanced at Perth, standing next to his father, watching them. "I'm so sorry I made you worry like this. But...well, I've changed my mind."

Rick stared at her, obviously gauging her words to make sure she was telling him the truth. Hannah joined them.

"Oh, these teenagers," she said good-naturedly. She brushed a kiss on his cheek. "And after all these years, you're finally here."

He reached out and tugged on a lock of Killian's hair and brushed her cheek with the back of his hand.

"Yeah, teenagers. I guess I should have known better." He turned to Hannah. "So this is your little corner of heaven. Think you can put up with me for a couple of days?"

Killian took his hand excitedly. It had been a long time since the two of them had spent any time together.

"Yes, we can. And we can even spare a cot for you to sleep on in the living room. Don't you think?" she asked Killian.

"Dad. There are some people I'd like you to meet."

Killian walked him over to the cottage and introduced him to Walt and Elena. She then turned to Perth.

"Perth Jonson," he said politely, stretching out his hand.

"Rick Fitch." He shook the younger man's hand, and Killian watched him looking cautiously into Perth's eyes. "And let me guess. You're the reason why my daughter had to leave yesterday...and you're also the reason why she wants to stay on the island now."

"Yes, sir. That would be me."

"Okay," he said warily. "Then I guess we need to talk, son."

AUTHOR'S NOTE

Aquarian is the first of three novels that will follow Killian's involvement with Perth, with the people of the island, and with the mythic forces that control life, death, and the future of the Aquarians.

The origin of this story lies in myth, but it also comes from our visits to the real island of Cuttyhunk, Massachusetts. This magical place took hold of our imagination from the first moment we rode the ferry into the island's harbor. Of course, *our* Cuttylea Island is entirely fictional. But who knows what lies beneath the grey waters beyond those rocky shores…

If you enjoyed *Aquarian*, be sure to visit our website or friend us on Facebook, and get on the mailing list for news of the second book in the series:

> www.JanCoffey.com

And in the meantime, we hope you'll try our other young adult stories, including our May McGoldrick novel *Tess and the Highlander*, as well as our Jan Coffey book *Tropical Kiss*.

We love hearing from our readers. Write to us at:

> JanCoffey@JanCoffey.com

Read on for previews of

May McGoldrick's

Tess and the Highlander

&

Jan Coffey's

Tropical Kiss

May McGoldrick's

TESS AND THE HIGHLANDER

CHAPTER 1

The Isle of May, off the Firth of Forth

Scotland, March 1543

Tess poked at the corpse with a stick and backed away.

Her unbound auburn hair, already soaked from the driving rain, whipped across her eyes when she leaned in to look closer.

The Highlander appeared to be dead, but she couldn't be sure. Long, dark blond hair lay matted across his face. She looked at the high leather boots, darkened by the salt water. The man was wearing a torn shirt that once must have been white. A broad expanse of plaid, pinned at one shoulder by a silver brooch, trailed into the tidal pool. From the thick belt that held his kilt in place, a sheathed dirk banged against an exposed thigh.

A dozen seals watched her from the deep water beyond the surf.

With the storm growing increasingly wilder, she stood indecisively over the body. In all the years she'd been on the island, she'd never seen a human wash up before. Certainly, there had been wrecks in the storms that swept in across the open water, and Auld Charlotte and Garth used to find all kinds of things—some valuable and some worthless—cast up on the shores. Never, though, had there been another person—at least, not since the aging husband and wife had found Tess herself eleven years earlier.

Tess pushed aside those thoughts now and crouched beside the man, placing a hand hesitantly on his chest. A faint pounding beneath the shirt was the answer to her prayers...and her fears. She didn't want anyone intruding on her island and in her life. At the same time, she could not allow a living thing to die when she could save it. Or him.

The surf crashed over the ring of rock that formed the tidal pool, and the young woman pushed herself to her feet. She drew the leather cloak up to shield her face from the stinging spray of wind-driven brine. When she looked back at the body, the wave had pushed the Highlander deeper into the pool, immersing his face.

Tess immediately dropped her stick and lifted his face out of the water. Glancing over her shoulder, she eyed a flat rock at the far side of the pool. It sat higher than the tide generally rose. Rolling him forward slightly, she held him under the arms just as another wave crested the pool's rim. The surge of water lifted the body, and Tess quickly dragged him through the water toward the rock.

He was heavier than she thought he would be. Out of breath, she finally succeeded in getting him partially anchored on the rock.

Auld Charlotte had once told Tess that they'd found her nearly drowned in this same tidal pool. The thought of that now flickered in her mind. She tried to recall the storm and the ship and the day, but those memories had long ago faded into nightmares. Now, it was all buried too deeply within her to recollect. She wondered if it was a day like this one.

The dirk at the Highlander's side caught her eye, and Tess reached down quickly, yanked the weapon from its sheath, and tucked it into her own belt.

The wind was howling, and the salt spray was stinging her face. Tess looked out at the frothy, gray-green sea, hoping to see some boat searching for the Highlander lying unconscious beside her.

If they came, she wouldn't let herself be seen, though. She wanted no news of her presence be carried to the mainland.

She had only been six years old when the ship had sank and she had washed ashore. But the little she allowed herself to remember from the time before that day was too painful. Tess had no desire to face that horrifying past ever again. There was no place else that she ever wanted to be but here. This island was the only home she had left.

For eleven years, the reclusive couple had kept her existence a secret. And now, with both of them dead, she could only pray to continue her life as before, undisturbed.

Her plan was the same as the one she'd followed dozens of times since washing up on this island. Whenever there was a chance of a fishing boat or some pilgrims coming ashore, Garth and Charlotte would trundle Tess off with plenty of food and blankets to the caves on the western shore of the island. She would remain there in safety until all was well and the visitors were gone.

The only difference now was that she would have to use her own judgment about when it would be safe to come out.

Ready to push herself to her feet, a tinge of curiosity made Tess reach and push the Highlander's wet hair out of his face. Instantly, she was sorry for the action, for the man's features took her by surprise. Even unconscious, or perhaps because of it, he was an extremely handsome man. A high forehead, a straight nose, a face devoid of the beard that she'd assumed all Highlanders wore. He had a face not even marred by scars…yet. Only a few scratches and bruises from his time in the surf.

Angry for allowing herself to be distracted, she started to get to her feet, but one foot slipped, and she had to brace a hand on his chest to catch herself.

His eyes immediately opened, and Tess's breath knotted tightly in her chest. Blue eyes the color of a winter sky stared at her from beneath long dark lashes flecked with gold. She didn't blink. She didn't move. Holding her breath, she remained still for the eternity of a moment until he closed them again.

She edged off the rock and ran as fast and as far as her legs would take her.

Jan Coffey's

TROPICAL KISS

CHAPTER 1

June, Aruba

He was late.

The heat was giving Morgan Callahan a headache. She looked at the long afternoon rays of Caribbean sun sliding toward her along the sidewalk. The bench she was sitting on occupied one of the few areas of shade remaining on the stretch of white concrete outside the airport terminal. Sun was poison on her freckled Boston Irish skin. She avoided it like the plague.

How much longer could he be? she thought, looking at her watch.

God, it was hot.

Morgan glanced over her shoulder at the sliding glass doors leading from the air-conditioned baggage claim area. When she'd stepped out of the plane an hour ago, it seemed like the entire population of Aruba was packed into that area. Now she knew why. The air was crisp. The white floors shining. Even the green plants in the raised dividers looked happy and healthy. And cool.

But she hadn't stayed inside. Hobbling on her crutches and pulling her bags behind her, she had come out ahead of most of the tourists.

She knew now she'd expected too much. Wished for the impossible. She'd thought Philip might just be there to pick her up. Waiting for her.

Fat chance.

Aruba's airport was not exactly as busy as Boston's Logan. The flight Morgan had come in on had been the only one arriving for that hour. There were no lines for immigration, no multiple conveyer belts running to process people's luggage. Everything came through quickly and without a hitch, it seemed. In and out within fifteen minutes. She'd stood in line longer to get a Happy Meal. A stamp on the passport and everyone was off to hotels and timeshares and whatever.

Morgan looked across the empty taxi stand at the rental car buildings across the way. The sun was blinding on the whitewashed concrete buildings. The entire place seemed deserted.

She breathed in the smells of baked Caribbean cement and jet exhaust. Gross.

Beyond the entrance to the airport, everywhere she looked, the heat was giving the island that hazy, miragy look. She could see in the distance, rising sharply above the flat surrounding area, one high round hill with a little white building on top.

"Come on, Philip," she muttered, tapping her good foot on the pavement.

The sweat was trickling down the inside of the cast on her leg, and the itching was about to drive her crazy. Thank God she'd at least been smart enough to wear a light sundress. She lifted the limp blanket of hair off her neck. It didn't help. There was no breeze to cool her skin. She tied her hair back into a pony tail.

She thought of the magazine she'd read on the plane from Boston. *The trade winds keep the island cool with year-round breezes.* Yeah, right.

Morgan leaned over and tried to get a finger down inside her cast. Why was it that the itch was always just a little further down than she could reach? She pulled off her sunglasses and used one of the handles. She still couldn't reach. The sun had finally reached her, and the rays were crawling up her legs. She gave up, gritted her teeth, and pulled on her shades.

Behind her the sliding doors opened and she glanced around at them. A short, middle-aged guy came out. Straw Indiana Jones hat, khakis, a large untucked Hawaiian shirt. Morgan remembered seeing him on the plane. He'd been wearing his hat even then. Later on, as everyone was going up the ramp toward the Aruban customs area, he was walking a couple of steps ahead of her. He had a nose that looked like it had been chewed on by something and the tan, leathery skin of someone who worked in construction or who had spent lots of hours in the sun, anyway. He also didn't look like he was too hot on shaving. His chin could have easily been mistaken for the butt of some aging porcupine.

Looking at him now, Morgan had no idea about his nationality. She knew he wasn't American, though; she'd noticed that he had a different color passport when he was heading to customs ahead of her.

As the doors closed behind him, he pulled out a pack of cigarettes and lit one. He was carrying only a briefcase. She glanced at her two suitcases, the backpack, and her purse. Mistake. She didn't know what the heck she'd been thinking to pack so much stuff.

Like she was ever going to leave the house during the couple of months that she was stuck here in Aruba.

She got a whiff of his smoke and immediately became annoyed. The last thing she needed was to have her asthma flare up. There was no air here as it was. Wheezing wouldn't be fun. He saw her looking at him. He smiled and started over toward her.

Great, she thought. *American girl abducted from deserted Aruba airport.*

"*Bon tardi,*" he said.

"I don't speak…uh, Dutch?" she guessed, not really knowing what language he'd just spoken.

"Papiamento," he corrected. "The native tongue of Aruba."

"You're Aruban?"

"From the islands."

That wasn't much of an answer. There were lots of islands in the Caribbean.

He puffed on his cigarette and pushed back the rim of his hat. "American?"

Wasn't it tattooed on her forehead?

"Yeah," she said, glad that she'd spread out her backpack and luggage on the bench. There was no room for him to sit down next to her.

"Your first time in Aruba?"

Morgan wished she could lie. The way he was looking at her was creeping her out. His eyes were kind of squinty, like he was sizing up some ripe cantaloupe.

"First time," she said, looking off toward the road. Two cars turned in from the main highway, but neither came toward the terminal doors.

"Boyfriend picking you up?"

"Not boyfriend." She kicked herself after saying it. She didn't have to explain.

"Traveling by yourself?"

"No," she said right away. "Visiting family. Visiting my father. He lives on the island."

"Works for the oil company?"

"No."

He took another drag from the cigarette and blew the smoke in her direction. "Hotel business. Casino supervisor."

"No." She pulled the crutches closer to her. They were the only two people out there on the sidewalk. She looked over her shoulder at the sliding glass doors of the airport building. The sun's reflection on them prevented her from seeing inside. She had no clue if anyone was even in there.

"Construction."

"No," she answered under her breath. He'd moved to where the bright yellow sun was behind him. She could no longer see his face because of the shadow. She decided to turn the tables on him. "Is someone picking you up?"

"How about if I give you a ride?"

"No. Thank you," she said tersely, guessing that he wasn't going to be much for answering questions. Still, she thought, a good defense was the best offense…or the other way around. Whatever. "Do you have a car?"

He held one hand out, palm up…like he was checking for rain. "What kind of man would I be if I had no car?"

"Then why don't you go get in your car and get out of here."

"You can come with me."

"No," she said louder and more pointedly. "My father is coming to get me."

She could tell he was grinning at her. He dropped his cigarette on the clean sidewalk and crushed it out.

"No oil business, no hotels or casinos, no construction. I say you lie about your father. I think your boyfriend is standing you up. You come with me. I'll show you real island life."

For the first time, fear clutched at her gut. She was in a foreign country. The airport had turned into a ghost town. She had no cell phone. Great.

Not that there was anyone she could call here anyway, considering the fact that Philip had apparently forgotten she was coming to visit. Morgan looked over her shoulder at the doors again. The heck with her luggage. Maybe she could get inside. There had to be somebody...

"They locked the doors when I came out," he said following the direction of her glance. "They want nobody going in that way."

Porcupine Butt picked up her backpack and dropped it on the sidewalk, making room for himself.

He sat, she stood. It was like seesaw. She grabbed her crutches and tucked them under her arms. She wasn't familiar with the airport, didn't know where the other entrances were, but there was no reason for him to sense her fear.

"*Unda bo ta bai?*"

"English, please."

"Where are you going?" He patted the seat next to him. "Sit down. Visit with me."

"I don't think so." She hobbled backward a step. "I like to be left alone. Please go."

"Pretty girl like you shouldn't be left alone."

Morgan's temper started to push past her fear.

"I don't know what your problem is, but I told you I'm waiting for my father...and he happens to be a high-ranking official for the United States government. He's here in Aruba on assignment, and he has important friends in high places. Very high places." Morgan didn't think it was necessary to say that, from what she could tell, Philip Callahan had spent his entire, boring, low-level, bureaucratic life behind a desk, pushing paper for those important people. "He should be here any minute. So unless you're looking for trouble, you'd better just leave me alone and be on your way."

The sound of a car speeding into the airport from the road jerked Morgan's head around. Immediately, her stomach sank. A new black Jaguar with tinted windows was racing toward them. She backed another step away from the curb as the car came up and screeched to a stop. She could hear Jay-Z blasting, even with the windows closed.

Somehow, Morgan doubted that Philip was in that car.

"You wait for your father. I wait for my nephew." Old Porcupine Butt was smiling as he got to his feet.

The driver revved the engine of the Jag. Even this close, Morgan couldn't see how many people were inside.

"Come with us?"

She shook her head and continued to back away. Her mind was racing. There could be two of them in the Jag, maybe three. They could force her into the car with them. She was liking this less and less. The rap music suddenly stopped.

As the car door started to open, she felt someone put a hand on her shoulder. Gasping, she whirled around and swung one of her crutches hard. The wood connected solidly with the knee of the man behind her. She heard him curse out aloud and stagger backwards.

Right away, Morgan had a strong suspicion that she might have aimed wrong. The young man holding his knee was dressed in khakis, a white polo shirt, and loafers with no socks. All and all, he looked too preppy to be very threatening, in spite of the continuing stream of muttered curses. She saw him bend over and snatch his sunglasses from the sidewalk where they'd fallen. When he looked at her, there was murder in his eyes.

"What was that for?"

"You grabbed me. It was self-defense."

"Self-defense?" he said, scowling. "I touched you on the shoulder. You weren't watching where you were going. You were backing right into me."

"You materialized out of thin air."

"I came out the side door of the terminal," he replied. "These doors were locked."

He was tall and had a nice build. Actually, Morgan was pretty impressed with herself for being able to knock him back a step. His brown hair was longish and straight. Handsome, but definitely too serious. At least, right now he looked pretty serious.

Morgan figured his ego had taken a bigger hit than his knees. He was still flexing his knee, but other than that he didn't seem to be in too much pain.

"It's not nice to sneak up on people," she said under her breath.

"I wasn't sneaking up on you. You backed into me." His green eyes disappeared behind the sunglasses. "You're not even going to apologize?"

"I'm sorry," she told him. "But it wasn't like I hit you intentionally."

Morgan jumped at the sound of the car door slamming. As she turned, the Jag took off in the direction of the main road. Thankfully, her annoying friend was nowhere to be seen. She'd had enough excitement. She'd just wait inside the terminal.

She hobbled back to the bench, grabbed her purse, picked up the backpack, and slung the two items onto her shoulder. The strap of the purse caught on one of the crutches. She tried to unhook it, but the backpack slipped off her shoulder, knocking over the two suitcases like a pair of dominoes. As she reached down to straighten them up, her sunglasses fell off the bridge of her nose. She tried to catch them, but the purse—still tangled up with the crutch—stopped her. Morgan pulled the purse off her arm and took a step back, glaring at the items in front of her.

"Behave," she muttered at the tangled mess of items at her feet.

"You *must* be Morgan Callahan."

Complete Book List as of 2012

Writing as Jan Coffey:

AQUARIAN
THE BLIND EYE
THE PUPPET MASTER
THE DEADLIEST STRAIN
THE PROJECT
SILENT WATERS
FIVE IN A ROW
TROPICAL KISS
FOURTH VICTIM
TRIPLE THREAT
TWICE BURNED
TRUST ME ONCE

Writing as May McGoldrick:

GHOST OF THE THAMES
ARSENIC AND OLD ARMOR
MADE IN HEAVEN
DREAMS OF DESTINY
CAPTURED DREAMS
BORROWED DREAMS
THE REBEL
TESS AND THE HIGHLANDER
THE PROMISE
THE FIREBRAND
THE ENCHANTRESS
THE DREAMER
FLAME
THE INTENDED
BEAUTY OF THE MIST
HEART OF GOLD
ANGEL OF SKYE
THISTLE AND THE ROSE

Writing as Nikoo Kafi:

OMID'S SHADOW

ABOUT THE AUTHOR

Jan Coffey and May McGoldrick are just two pen names that adorn the covers of Nikoo and Jim McGoldrick's books. With an engineering degree, a PhD in British literature, and experiences ranging from the clubs of Rodeo Drive to the shipyards of New England to the college classrooms of Pennsylvania, these two writers together have created over thirty books, have won numerous awards, and have touched the hearts of countless readers. When it comes to pursuing their dreams, they are the little engine that could.

www.JanCoffey.com

CPSIA information can be obtained
at www.ICGtesting.com
Printed in the USA
BVHW041818250420
578485BV00012B/376